C. L.

I can't do this. I can't do this.

"Can it be? Elijah Miller? After all these years?"

"It is." He struggled to speak. Seeing her after all this time had sucked the air from his lungs. "How are you, Hannah?"

She tilted her head to the side, her grin widening. "How long have you been home? I haven't heard a word about your visit."

"I just arrived, actually." He forced out each word carefully. Painfully.

A buzzing sound zipped through the air between them, and suddenly all of Eli's wavering uncertainty vanished. It sounded like the crack of a weapon. Eli turned his head to the woods behind him. *Was that gunfire?*

He dived forward, covering Hannah with his body and forcing her to the ground. Eleven years working the city streets had taught him to react first and think later.

A second buzzing flew over them. A nanosecond later, the front window of the house shattered.

Oh, yeah. That was gunfire.

Books by Kit Wilkinson

Love Inspired Suspense

Protector's Honor
Sabotage
Plain Secrets

Love Inspired

Mom in the Making

KIT WILKINSON

is a former Ph.D. student who once wrote discussions on the medieval feminine voice. She now prefers weaving stories of romance and redemption. Her first inspirational manuscript won a prestigious RWA Golden Heart and her second has been nominated for an *RT Book Reviews* Reviewer's Choice Award. You can visit Kit at www.kitwilkinson.com or write to her at write@kitwilkinson.com.

PLAIN SECRETS

Kit Wilkinson

Love Inspired

Recycling programs for this product may not exist in your area.

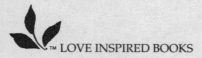

™ LOVE INSPIRED BOOKS

ISBN-13: 978-0-373-67520-3

PLAIN SECRETS

This edition published by arrangement with Love Inspired Books.

® and TM are trademarks of Love Inspired Books, used under license. Trademarks indicated with ® are registered in the United States Patent and Trademark Office, the Canadian Trade Marks Office and in other countries.

www.LoveInspiredBooks.com

Printed in U.S.A.

Live a life worthy of the Lord and please him
in every way: bearing fruit in every good work,
growing in the knowledge of God,
being strengthened with all power according to his
glorious might so that you may have great endurance
and patience.... For he has rescued us from the
dominion of darkness and brought us
into the kingdom of the Son he loves, in whom
we have redemption, the forgiveness of sins.
—*Colossians* 1:10–14

To my sister, Elizabeth Ann,
whose faith never falters. Thanks for all the support,
love and direction over the years.

And

To my editor, Elizabeth,
for her patience and guidance. Danke. Merci. Gracias.
Arigato… I really cannot thank you enough :-)

ONE

Where is that girl? Hannah Nolt could hardly believe her seventeen-year-old stepdaughter had spent the entire night away from home. But here it was morning as sure as the rooster crowed in the new day, and not a single sign that Jessica had come home.

Hannah stepped from the warmth of the cottage, bracing for the chill of morning air. She tried to ward off all negative conclusions about the girl she'd raised as her own. It wasn't like her to stay out all night even on *Rumspringa*—that time when Amish youth have their "run around." And shirking morning duties was never a part of that.

Hannah should have been angry with Jessica, but instead it was only worry that filled her bones as she shivered in the darkness on her way to morning milking.

Jessica had been acting strangely for weeks now—demanding privacy, running off for hours with no explanation, even leaving the farm on weeknights. Things she had never done before. Hannah did not question the change in her behavior. She and Jessica had been closer than ever since Hannah's husband's death, just two years ago, and she had faith in Jessica's good sense and kind spirit. Surely these estranged few weeks were just a simple bump in the road—a growing pain, nothing to be alarmed over. Now Hannah wondered if perhaps she had been wrong to put so much trust in the girl.

Hannah rushed on to the barn. Maybe Jessica had gone straight there from wherever she'd been all night.

Maybe.

But as she scurried up the steep hill, her hope that Jessica was inside milking the Jersey heifers diminished. Fear as thick as the morning fog clouded her thoughts. Something was wrong. Something terribly, horribly wrong. She could feel it in her bones. None of this made sense. Jessica was not the kind of girl to stay out late, much less all night. She just wouldn't do such a thing. Not by choice. No. Something had happened. Something *Farrichterlick—frightful*. She closed her eyes and lifted her head to the skies. *Please let her be safe, Lord. Let her be safe.*

Hannah turned back to the path. A bright flash grazed the hillside, then disappeared. She paused.

What is that? A coming storm? She heard no thunder. Saw no clouds.

Her dread doubled as she climbed the last slope to the barn. She pushed open the back door and stepped inside. Another flash of light blinded her eyes. It speared through the inside of the stable. That was no storm. *Those were car lights.*

The *vroom, vroom* of a powerful engine broke through the silent morning air. Hannah's heart raced. Her mouth went dry. Who could be at the barn at this hour of the day? She shuddered. Whatever the reason, it could not be good.

She lifted her lantern. Cold air whooshed around her. Had someone just passed her? Brushed against her?

"Hallo? Jessica? Is that you?" The dead space swallowed her voice. Not even the animals responded. Another flush of air brushed around her. The door behind her slammed shut. She turned, only to have the lantern knocked from her hands. Its flame was extinguished as it hit the dirt floor. As she scrambled after it, something bumped against her once more, this time knocking her to all fours.

Please, God. Be my light. Help me to safety.

Scrambling to her feet again, Hannah lunged toward the closed door, but the large wooden slider wouldn't budge. She was trapped. The only other door out was at the other side, where she'd seen the car lights. Where she still heard its engine. She took one step forward and stopped. She had not the courage. Sliding into an empty stall, she crouched low, pressing her back against the wall. Footsteps padded down the aisle behind her. Hard, heavy steps—those of a man, a large man. The man who had locked her in and knocked her to the floor.

Beams of light once again filled the eaves of the barn. Hannah sucked in her breath and pressed deeply into the wooden boards behind her, wishing somehow she could disappear into the wall.

Please be leaving. Whoever, whatever you are…please be leaving.

A car door slammed. Gravel crunched. The hum of the car motor grew dim. Her prayer had been answered. She slinked upward and peered over the edge of the stall. Through the open front doors, Hannah spotted a long, shiny black sedan heading away.

Hoping but not truly believing she was alone, she crouched again, feeling over the earthen floor for her dropped lantern. She refilled her lungs, taking in the soothing, familiar smells of animal and hay. She tried to calm her panicked mind. She listened to the cows' lows and sheep's vibrating *baas*.

With trembling hands, she found her lantern

and relit the flame. A warm orange glow filled the space around her, and her eyes adjusted to the soft light.

Slowly, she stood and stumbled her way to the front of the stable. Her mind reeled. What had just happened? Who had pushed her to the ground and locked her inside, and why? What mischief had brought an *Englischer*'s car to their barn? Hannah's legs trembled under her as she moved across the dirt floor. She jumped when one of the cows swung her head into the aisle, then again when the gray barn cat sauntered over her path.

"The Lord is my shepherd. I shall not fear." Hannah whispered the Psalm to herself and the animals. *I should not be so frightened.* She wondered if the disturbance had something to do with Jessica's absence. In fact, for a moment the car had given her hopes that Jessica had come home. But that idea had died when she was locked in and knocked to the floor.

The cat cried. Hannah stooped to scratch its head. A lamb skirted beside her, down the aisle and out the front.

"What are you doing loose, little girl?" Hannah placed her lantern on the ledge of the sheep pen. Someone had left the gate wide. She peered in only to see that the space was mostly empty. Twenty-plus sheep were out scampering the hillside no doubt. Once it was light, she'd fetch one of the dogs to help round them up.

Hannah turned back to the aisle but stopped as something in the far corner caught her eye. One sheep still sleeping. How odd that he hadn't stirred when the others roused. Perhaps he was hurt. She reached back for her lantern and moved nearer with care not to startle the creature. But as she closed in on the figure, she realized it was no animal. It was a human. A girl. An Amish girl. Her Amish girl.

Hannah knelt beside her stepdaughter, who in all this time had not moved, nor made a sound.

"Jessica? Jessica?"

Putting the lantern aside once again, she touched the girl's shoulders and rolled her slightly, drawing her face toward herself.

Jessica's body was cold. And there was blood. On her face. On her apron. On her neck and hands.

Jessica! Jessica! Oh, Father in Heaven, what has happened?

Hannah whispered prayers as she felt the lifelessness of the body beside her. Shock flowed over her and flashes of Peter erupted into her thoughts. Images of the night he'd been killed. The ice. The untrained horse. The car coming him, traveling too fast. Her dear husband, Jessica's father, thrown from the buggy and trampled. There had been much blood that night, as well.

Hannah reached for the girl's arm to feel for a pulse. There was none. No life. No spirit. Jessica was no longer in this body. No longer with her.

She touched the girl's cheeks and turned her face toward the light. There on her soft neck hung open flesh. The throat had been cut—deliberately. The marks were deep. A wound as deadly as the one her father had taken just two years ago.

"The Lord giveth and the Lord taketh away. Blessed be the name of the Lord." Hannah whispered the familiar words from Job then fell over the girl's body and wept.

"Yo! Miller."

Elijah Miller, Philadelphia Internal Affairs detective, swung his head in the direction of Captain O'Dell's deep voice.

"Need to speak with you. Pronto." The captain gestured toward his office.

Elijah pushed away from his desk. His partner, Mitchell Tucci, stood, too, and started to follow.

"Not you, Tucci. Just Miller."

Eli jerked his head around to glance back at his partner, who shrugged. It was rarely a good thing when the captain called you to his office. *Never* a good thing if he called you in by yourself. Elijah crisscrossed his way through the maze of desks and entered O'Dell's corner space.

"Shut the door. Take a seat," his captain said.

Eli did as he was told. O'Dell flung a pile of five-by-seven evidence photos across the desk. "The Lancaster police sent these over. Their chief wants your help with a homicide."

"Why would they want me on a homicide? I'm Internal Affairs."

When the captain didn't answer, he looked down at the first picture. A dead teenaged girl. She wore a frock and an apron and a prayer *Kapp*. A wave of nausea coursed through his veins. This was no normal homicide. This was an *Amish* homicide.

"Where in Lancaster is she from?" he asked.

"Willow Trace."

His hometown. Elijah's teeth clenched. His mind raced with the images of old faces, friends and family. He shuffled to the next picture. *A stable*. And the next. *Her slit throat*. The next. *Bruises and cuts*.

When he'd gone through the entire stack, he placed the pictures back on the edge of the desk and tried to keep down his breakfast of toast and black coffee. Silence filled the room. Eli stared at the floor, trying to squeeze the horrid images from his mind. But he couldn't stop his racing thoughts. Who was this girl? A neighbor? A friend's daughter? He pitied the family. Mourned for them. Then wondered at the idea that they encouraged an investigation. Could that be possible? Had things changed that much since he'd left home? The Amish didn't usually encourage any sort of police aid—or interference, as they thought of it. They liked to take care of their own problems. Eli didn't imagine this community trait had altered since he'd lived there.

"You okay?" the captain asked.

Eli shook his head. "I don't want to work an Amish homicide.... She could be a relative."

"She's not. I checked. Her name is Jessica Nolt." O'Dell grabbed a page from the tiny file folder and began to read. "Daughter of Peter Nolt. Also deceased. Lived with stepmother Han—"

"Hannah Kurtz Nolt." Eli's voice was cold as he pronounced that name for the first time in a decade.

"Oh, you know these people?"

"Yes. My family shares a property line with them. I knew Peter well. He was a bit older than me. I was friends with his younger brother. And Hannah..." His throat closed tighter. "Hannah was my girlfriend." *Once upon a time...in a far-away land.*

"Girlfriend?" The captain looked skeptical.

Eli swallowed hard. "Yep. I dated Hannah while she worked as a nanny to Peter's daughter.

Peter's first wife died soon after giving birth to Jessica—a bad case of hepatitis. Peter was devastated. Hannah's parents sent her to help the Nolt family."

"Then daddy fell for the nanny?"

Eli shrugged; he did not like having that heartache rubbed in his face even after eleven years. "Something like that. Hannah started working for the family when she was twelve. The Nolts became her family—marriage just made it official. And Jessica was a very sweet girl. I remember her well." He shook away the memories—both good and bad. "So, how old was she? Fifteen? Sixteen?"

"Seventeen."

Seventeen. He frowned, thinking how an unexplained death like this would affect all of the community. And especially Hannah. "I see a deep laceration on her throat in this picture, but there's no blood. Not even on her clothes. This isn't the crime scene? Or has it been cleaned up?"

"I thought you didn't want to work the case."

"I don't. But I can't help being a little curious."

"The notes here explain that the uncle, Thomas Nolt, called Chief McClendon, but by the time he arrived, the family had already changed the girl's clothes and burned them. They claim there was no blood around her, only on her clothes. If they are telling the truth I think we can assume she wasn't killed in the stable."

"They are telling the truth…. What's the story on the girl?"

"A perfectly good girl, as far as the family tells it. No evidence of drugs or alcohol."

"But the family wouldn't necessarily know what she's involved in. She was probably on *Rumspringa*. Kids don't have to tell their parents anything much during that time." Eli sighed and glanced again at the horrid photos. "There's bruising on her arms and neck in those pictures. A struggle before death? Abuse? I can't imagine it of the Nolt family, but there are cases of abuse in the Amish community."

"I don't know. This is all we have." The captain held up the thin file. "The only other information in here is that her stepmother, Hannah, is the one who found her in the milking stable. Maybe you could start by questioning her."

Question Hannah? The woman who dumped me. No way. No Hannah. No Willow Trace. No investigation. "I don't think that's a good idea."

"Oh, come on. You don't have to be official about it. Just go and pay respects or whatever."

"Why me? If you just want someone to figure out what's going on, why not one of the local guys?"

"Chief McClendon says his own men aren't

always Amish-friendly. He'd heard of you, the Amish cop in the city, and thought the people would respond better with one of their own asking the questions."

Eli shook his head—that made no sense. Very few people knew he was raised Amish. "They'd be even less likely to answer me—because they'd think I should know better than to ask. The Amish don't seek revenge or restitution or even answers for unexplained events. They accept it as God's will and move on. So they would have no reason to seek answers and therefore would have no interest in answering them. I can't imagine the family even wants an investigation."

"Well, they don't. That's why there was no autopsy. All we have are these pictures. And Chief McClendon took them himself. He thinks there's something major going on here and that you're our best shot at finding out what it is."

Eli shook his head. "I haven't seen these people in eleven years. I'm not one of them anymore. They won't talk to me about any of this. They probably don't even talk to each other about it."

The captain frowned. "McClendon thinks you'll have a chance."

Eli groaned. He did not want to go back to Willow Trace. Not now. Not ever. "I'm sorry, Captain. But I can't do this."

"You have to."

"But Tucci and I are right in the middle of a case against that officer in District Seven."

"I'll put someone else on it."

Eli shook his head. "You don't get it. I really cannot go back there."

"You have to." O'Dell folded up the record file. "I'll be honest with you, Miller, I don't quite get it, but this is *way* over my head."

Eli narrowed his eyes on the captain. "What? How can it be over your head from the Lancaster County police?"

His boss crossed his arms over his chest. "The request came from Chief McClendon via the governor."

"The governor?" Elijah stood and began to pace in front of his boss's desk. "How does the governor even know I exist?"

"No idea, Miller. But when the governor asks for you, you go."

An hour later, Eli was navigating the rolling hills of eastern Pennsylvania reluctantly on his way to Willow Trace. With every passing mile, the tension in him racked tighter and tighter. After eleven years, how would he be received? *Would* he be received? The only person who'd stayed in touch with him was his sister, Abigail. But even she did so in secret—their father, the local bishop, had told Elijah never to return if he chose to take up weapons as a part of his life and work.

Eli knew it was difficult for his family to understand the choice he'd made, not just to leave the community but to become a police officer. Yet the reasons for it went far back into his childhood. He'd only been about five years old when, during a trip to the city with his father, a crazy man on the train had kidnapped him and his sister, Abigail. If it had not been for the help of the Philadelphia police, Elijah and his sister would never have been reunited with their family. That incident had always made him admire and respect the police. When Hannah had chosen to marry Peter instead of him, Eli had felt certain that leaving the Amish community behind and becoming a policeman was what God had called him to do. Ironic that the very reason he'd never returned to Willow Trace since then was exactly the thing forcing him home today.

About as ironic as heading out to see Hannah—the woman he'd tried so hard to forget. They'd been so in love. Or at least he'd thought so. Then she'd married Peter. He'd felt like such a fool.

His thoughts rambled as he maneuvered his convertible through the hills and around the horse and buggies. He kept his head down and lifted a quick word. *Guard me from their judgment, Lord.*

If there is a job for me here, then make me strong
so I can do it. If not, let me return to what—

Eli looked up just in time to slam on the brakes
as another horse and carriage crossed right into
his lane while attempting to avoid a sleek black
sedan speeding around the buggy on the right
shoulder.

Crazy driver. Couldn't slow down one second
for a buggy. *Good grief.* Someone could have
been seriously injured. He shook his head, remembering all too well the days of being in the
buggy himself and having those sorts of inci-
dents. They happened more frequently than they
should. He patted the dash of his Mustang. He felt
much safer in his convertible.

Checking his rearview mirror, he searched for
the car, but the black sedan had already fled the
area. Thankfully, the horse and buggy were recovered and back on their side of the road. Eli
drove on.

Minutes later, he turned onto the dirt path leading to the Nolts' farmhouse. A chill of unease
rippled down his spine with the strangest feeling that he was being watched. He parked in the
gravel turnaround in front of the quaint two-story
stone cottage and stepped out of his car. The old
house hadn't changed. The sight of it flooded his
head with hundreds of memories—gatherings,
Sunday church, buggy rides.

A woman stepping onto the long white porch restored his mind to the present. She wore a blue frock with a black apron. Her raven hair had been tucked tightly away under a white prayer *Kapp*. She dried her hands on the skirt of her apron, then pressed away the creases, all the while studying him from the safety of the porch. At length, a soft, pleasant smile fell over her lips.

Hannah.

Eli froze to his spot on the front walkway. She was stunning as ever—her sweet face, her deep emerald eyes. As soft and beautiful as the last time he'd seen her so many years ago. She smiled wide, although from the redness around her eyes he guessed she'd been crying recently, no doubt over the loss of her daughter. Still, as she moved toward him, she was easy and natural. Seeing her felt like a cool breeze against his skin on the hottest of summer days. A lump the size of a stone grew into his throat, and his heart pumped four times its normal speed.

I can't do this. I can't do this.

"Can it be? Elijah Miller?" Her alto voice sounded smooth and rich. "After all these years?"

"It is." He struggled to speak. Seeing her again seemed to have sucked the air from his lungs and brought back so many memories his head was full. "How are you, Hannah?"

She tilted her head to the side, grinning wider.

"How long have you been home? I have not heard a word about your visit. How is that so?"

"I just arrived, actually." He forced out each word carefully. Painfully. He shifted his weight and pressed his lips together. Her friendliness surprised him a little but not as much as his own reaction. Where was all the pain and anger he should be feeling?

"And you have not been first to see your *Mamm?* How is that?"

A buzzing sound zipped through the air between them. Eli turned his head to the woods. *Was that gunfire?*

Suddenly all of his wavering uncertainty vanished. Years of training and experience had hardwired his response to that sound—even when it came at the most unlikely of moments. Without a second thought, he dove forward, covering Hannah with his body and forcing her to the ground. Eleven years working the city streets had taught him to react first and think later. A skill that had saved his life on more than one occasion.

A second buzzing flew over them. A nanosecond later, the front window of the house shattered.

Oh yeah. That was gunfire.

TWO

"What's going on?" Hannah tried to sit up and take stock of the situation. Elijah pushed her back to the ground.

"Stay down. Someone's shooting at us." He rolled onto his back and pulled his Glock from its shoulder holster, aiming it toward the woods.

Hannah stared wide-eyed at his gun. She scooted back a few feet, then started to stand.

"What are you doing?" He jumped up after her, shielding her body again but continuing to face the woods with his firearm cocked and ready. "You're making yourself a target. Those are real bullets, Hannah."

"*Jah,* all the more reason to move inside, no?" She hurried toward the porch.

Okay. Maybe she had a point.

Eli covered her as they made their way to the front door. He kept his eyes on the edge of the nearby forest. "Is anyone else home?"

She shook her head.

"I'll go first." He slipped in front of her and into the house, gun raised. Glass from the broken window had sprayed out across the hardwood floor. Otherwise, the large open space looked untouched. He pulled her in behind him and placed her in a corner away from the open door and window.

"Stay here while I check upstairs and in the *Dawdi Haus*."

Hannah nodded. Eli ran up the stairs. He checked the bedrooms and single bath of the main cottage. He opened the connecting door leading to the *Dawdi* or grandparent addition and hurried through the small, attached living space. The entire place was empty.

"Clear." He descended to the living room. Hannah was still crouched in the corner. He put away his gun and knelt in front of her. "I'm going to search the woods. Don't move until I get back."

"You're going back out there?" Her eyes widened.

He placed his hands on her shoulders, trying to catch one of her nervous glances, but her eyes would not rest. She shook all over. And he didn't blame her. Someone had just blown out her front window. He hated to leave her, but he had to check the woods. "I'll be right back. And I'll keep an eye on the house the whole time."

She nodded, her body still trembling and her

eyes avoiding his. But he could see the tears in them. As her head sank lower, Elijah's heart dropped. He hated the fear she was feeling on top of the pain she'd already been through. This wasn't the time for condolences, but the words burst out anyway.

"I'm sorry about your daughter. I'm sorry about Jessica."

He quietly slid through the front door and took off across the front lawn, finding cover behind an unfinished wooden shed, his car, then an old stone well. His mind spun hard and fast with muddled questions and strange emotions...and Hannah. And he didn't like any of it one bit.

At the forest edge, Eli did his best to estimate the position of the shooter and he scanned for any evidence—a footprint, a thread of material, bullet casings. Anything besides a plethora of flora and fauna. But there was nothing, not even a squirrel skittering about. So when a twig snapped behind him, he immediately turned and raised his gun.

He lowered it just as quickly. A small child stood there—an Amish child, dressed in a blue shirt, black trousers with suspenders and a straw hat.

"Sorry." Eli clicked on the safety of his gun and slid the piece back into its holster. "Don't be afraid. I thought you were someone else."

The boy frowned and pointed through the woods. "He went that way."

"Who went that way?"

"You look for man with, uh, *der Pistole?*" The boy looked at the Glock.

"You saw the man with the gun?"

The boy nodded and pulled his hand from behind his back to reveal a large black hat, the kind the Amish men wore.

"The man was Amish?" Eli's voice cracked with surprise.

The boy shook his head. "*Nein.* English he was."

"But he wore this hat?"

"*Jah.* He wear hat but also he have a...*Oberlippenbart.*" The boy pointed to his upper lip.

"A mustache?" Eli was thankful the kid was observant. No Amish man grew a mustache— only the beard. So, the kid was right. The shooter could not have been Amish. Not that it was likely a shooter was Amish anyway, as the People did not support the use of weapons—and hence the main reason his own father could not accept his choice of professions. "Did you see where he went?"

"In black car. Big black car." The boy's eyes were wide with admiration.

A black car? Like the one that nearly caused the wreck earlier? "And the car?"

"It goes."

Of course, the car was long gone, but at least he'd been searching in the right place. Whoever he was, he had taken his shell casings with him, meaning he was probably not an amateur. Although if he was a pro, and had been aiming at Eli or Hannah, then why had he missed? They'd been standing out in the open, without a thought of danger, until the first shot had been fired. Could his poor aim have been deliberate? Like warning shots? Eli looked back at the boy. "Okay, son. Let's get you home. Where do live?"

"Miller's Grove."

Elijah nodded. Miller's Grove was the home of his uncle. "What's your name, son?"

"Nicholas." He grinned. "Nicholas Miller."

"Well, you get on home, Nicholas Miller." Eli smiled at the child. "Can I have that hat?"

The boy lifted the hat to him. "Are you a policeman?"

"I am," Eli said, then watched the child, his very own cousin, scramble down the same path he'd taken so many times, so many years ago. At the other edge of the woods, an older girl with golden braids walked the path in her bare feet. No doubt it was Nicholas's sister come to fetch her brother home.

Elijah sighed and headed back to Nolt Cottage. *Great.* That cute cousin would head home now and tell all his siblings about the cop in the woods…and then everyone would know he was back in Willow Trace.

But would he be staying long enough to make a difference to his family? He wasn't sure yet. From those surprising first few minutes, it looked as though he was needed in Willow Trace—at least judging by the flying bullets. But even that didn't make him want to stay. Seeing Hannah had been strange enough. He couldn't imagine a confrontation with his own father. No. The sooner he was out of there, the better.

Hannah wrapped her arms around her legs, hugging her knees to her chest, as if she could squeeze away her own fears. But when her eyes fixed on the shards of broken glass spread across the floor, she continued to tremble.

Today had been the first time she'd dared be alone since that morning in the barn, since Jessica's "accident"—as Thomas, her brother-in-law, referred to the girl's death. But Hannah didn't believe Jessica's death was an accident. Dead bodies don't get placed in barns by accident. People probably don't shoot at you and your house accidentally, either. Losing Jessica had been devastating enough on its own—she had never once imagined that whatever had gotten Jessica killed could put herself or any others in danger, too.

Perhaps Thomas and she should not have kept silent about the events surrounding Jessica's death. About the blood and how she'd been away all night. About her many secrets. About the black car at the barn and the intruder who pushed Hannah down and locked her inside. If only she could relive that last week. As her mother, she could have prevented this. She should have prevented this.

In her mind she replayed the moments when she could have stopped Jessica and asked her what she was about. Each time she'd failed. What she would give to have just one more day with her precious daughter. Hannah dropped her head in a fit of sobs. What she would give not to have found her in the stable that morning. It seemed the more she tried to push away the memory of that morning, the more she relived it in her mind....

"Oh, Jessica, I'm so sorry. I'm so very sorry. If only I had been a better mother to you." Hannah had turned the girl's hands over in her own as she knelt beside her in the stall. The girl was so disheveled, bloodied, dirty. "This is all my fault. I should have known what you were about. Rumspringa *or not, I should have taken better care of you. I can never forgive myself."*

Hannah had brushed the dirt and loose hairs from the girl's face.

"What's the trouble?" A deep voice had sounded at the front of the barn.

It was Thomas. He must have wondered why she wasn't in the house making breakfast. She moved to the side so that he could see his niece in the sheep's bed of straw.

He froze, the color draining from his face. He rushed forward. "Is that—is that Jessica?"

Hannah met his dark eyes. "I—I found her here. She's dead, Thomas. Jessica is dead. I have failed her and Peter and God...and you."

"This is not your doing," he said. "You must not blame yourself. You were a gut mother to her, Hannah. As gut as her own mother could have been. As good as if you had given birth to her yourself."

His words were meant to comfort, but Hannah fell limp at the reminder of her infertility and the end of what was to be her only chance at motherhood. She just sat crying silently as Thomas placed Jessica's hands together on her belly and patted them.

"Our God is sovereign, Hannah. He alone is ruler and judge. We must accept what has happened. Be strong." He touched his hand to hers. "I will call the elders."

"No. Please. I don't want anyone to see her this way."

He had seen she could not be calmed. "Stay

with Jessica until I return. I will bring her clothes. I don't want Nana to see her this way, either. I will also have to call the police, Chief McClendon. He is sensitive to our ways."

"Yes. Call the police. They will find who did this to my precious Jessica. I will tell them about the car I saw, and—"

Thomas put a finger to her mouth to stop her speech. "You will tell them nothing, Hannah. You know it is not our way to search for answers. It is in God's hands. Promise me you will say nothing."

She promised. He was right, of course—investigating was not what the Amish did. But she couldn't help wishing, as impossible as it seemed, that someone would come and help her find the truth.

Footsteps sounded on the front porch and she stiffened, turning her face toward the door. Elijah's solid frame blocked the sun from the room, and his dark shadow covered her. Both startled and relieved, Hannah placed a hand over her mouth and released a tight breath.

"I'm sorry. That took longer than I expected. I didn't mean to startle you. Are you okay?" He entered the house slowly.

"I am okay." She nodded. "Did you see anyone?"

"Yes. But not the shooter. I saw a child. And

according to him, the man with the *Pistole* drove away in a big black car."

A black car? Like the one at the barn when she'd found Jessica? She swallowed hard. "A child?"

He nodded. "Nicholas Miller. My own cousin, I believe."

"He is. Son of your cousin John. He comes to see the young horses from time to time. Loves them, he does. He wasn't hurt, was he?"

"No. He's fine. Went home down the path. I watched him through the forest." He walked closer. His eyes narrowed on her. "Do you know something about a black car?"

"How would I know about a black car?" She tried to keep her voice steady, but Eli's penetrating eyes kept her on edge. "I pay no attention to such things."

Closing in the space remaining between them, he offered a hand to help her up. "You sure you're okay, Hannah?"

"*Ach*. It's not every day people run around Willow Trace with guns and bullets." She stood without his help, took a step back and tried to face him. But the intensity in his eyes made her more nervous than she already felt.

He walked back to the front door and checked that it was secure. She hoped that he had put away his gun. He must remember that guns were *verboten.* Although there was something—a dark object—in his hands. As he moved back to the kitchen, she saw that it was a black broad-rimmed hat like the one Amish men wore when they weren't working in the sun. She wanted to ask him where he'd gotten it, but there was a more pressing question at hand. "Do you intend to stay awhile?"

Eli frowned taking a look down at the hat, which he then tossed onto the tabletop. "No, I don't—just long enough to figure out what's going on. According to my little cousin, this hat belongs to our shooter."

"Sure." She lifted a brow and glared at him. "An Amish man with a gun. Shooting at my house. Maybe you've forgotten but we don't have or use guns."

He gave her a dissatisfied look. "Any joker off the street can buy one of these hats in a tourist shop or online."

Right. Hannah dropped her head.

"So, let's get started, shall we? Who is shooting at you and why?"

Eli didn't sound angry, but in his eyes, she could see how uncomfortable he was to be there, talking to her again. She told herself that that was why he was being so abrupt, so different from the boy she remembered. She also told herself—and tried to believe—that his detached tone didn't hurt.

"I have no idea." And that was the truth. "In fact, maybe that someone was shooting at you? Your life involves guns much more often than mine, does it not? Or maybe it was a hunter with a bad aim?"

He tilted his head to the other side. "Except that it's not hunting season. You said yourself no one around here owns a gun. And for the other possibility, well…if someone wanted to shoot at me they would have better opportunities than driving out to Lancaster County and aiming through the woods."

She let out a nervous laugh. "Then it must be a mistake. Who would shoot at me?"

"A mistake?" His face was grim as he pulled his pistol from under his jacket, did something with it that made some clicking sounds, then returned it to his side. He looked up at her again and clenched his jaw. "Two shots within inches of each other, that's no mistake."

Hannah turned away and continued to stall the conversation. "Your weapon should be outside."

"Someone just shot at you. The gun stays here with me where I can use it."

"Then maybe *you* should go." She lifted her head high as if to challenge him.

"Gladly, just as soon as you tell me what's going on around here."

"I do not know what you mean."

"I'm talking about your stepdaughter's death and someone shooting at you." He folded his hands over his chest. "I'm here to investigate what happened to Jessica."

His words sent a quiver over her lips, but she fought through it. She would not cry in front of Elijah Miller. "Again, you—you must be mistaken. There was not to be an investigation. There was...nothing to investigate."

Elijah tossed a photo on the table next to the black hat. "Her neck was cut. She's bruised all over. Four days later someone is shooting at you and you say there is nothing to investigate?"

"How did you get that?" She glanced at the photo, immediately recognizing the wound to her dear girl's neck. Grabbing at her stomach, she turned away. She must be strong. There was no need to involve Elijah in this.

"Chief McClendon of the Lancaster police." Eli removed the photo from the table and put it away in his jacket pocket. "He asked me to come here and see what I could find out."

"And what do you find so far?"

"I think there is something to investigate. I think you should talk to me. This is no game,

Hannah. You need to protect yourself. Someone is threatening you and your family. You cannot sit and be silent."

"I know you want to help. And it's very kind of you." She forced a smile. "But it's not our way. We will accept what has happened."

"It's *not* very kind of me. I don't want to be here one bit. But it's my job and I take that pretty seriously. Now please stop avoiding my questions and tell me how and when all this started."

She glanced at him and saw the frustration but also sorrow in his eyes. Like so many years ago when she told him she'd decided to marry Peter. Then, too, she had not told him the entire truth. Here she was again, keeping secrets. But she had promised and she must keep her word.

She fetched a broom and dustpan from the cupboard, and with short, quick strokes, she began to sweep the broken glass that covered the floor. "Even if there was more to the story, it does not change the fact that Jessica is gone. So what is there to investigate?"

"Perhaps something about this black car that you know about but don't know about?"

She continued to sweep, not looking his way. He watched her for a few moments, then moved next to her and gently took the broom and dustpan from her hand.

She still refused to look up as she said, "We are all fine. Really."

"Really? Someone just shot at your house. That doesn't seem so 'fine' to me. I haven't forgotten the way things work around here. I understand that you want to let go and accept what has happened. I'm not trying to stop that—in fact, you may be able to let go more easily if you know what happened. Don't you even care about who killed your stepdaughter?"

"Of course I care. I miss her every minute. She was everything to me." Hannah began to tremble again, but she would not give in to her emotions. She would not show such weakness of faith. "But knowledge does not bring peace and understanding. That comes only from God."

The back of his hand caressed her cheek. The warmth was comforting, and for a strange, fleeting second, she longed to fall into his arms and weep. Instead she turned away.

He stepped back. "I wish this wasn't why I was here. I'm so sorry. I know you raised Jessica as your own child. I can't imagine what you are feeling and after what happened to Peter…"

She looked up and he must have been able to read the surprise in her face.

"Abigail told me. As a midwife, she has a cell phone in order for her patients to contact her when they go into labor. We talk occasionally.

She told me about Peter." He pressed his lips together. "He was a good man, Hannah. If he hadn't been, I... Well, that was a long time ago. I didn't come here to rake up the past. You must want to know what happened Jessica. So please, come sit with me. Talk to me. Tell me about her. She must have been a wonderful good girl with you as her *Mamm*."

With all of the charisma and ease he'd possessed as a young man, Eli put the broom and dustpan aside and led her back to the kitchen table. But she did not take a seat.

"Perhaps we should go to the porch?" she suggested.

"I don't think the porch is a good place for you today." He pulled out a chair for her. After she sat, he removed his coat and hung it over the back of one of the other kitchen chairs and sat opposite her. His gun was still in the holster at his side.

"Have you forgotten everything, Elijah Miller? We don't have guns in our houses."

"Actually, it's you who has forgotten that someone shot at you only fifteen minutes ago." He smiled and patted the gun under his arm. "It's staying right where it is."

"Nana Ruth will be horror-struck."

"Nana Ruth will never know." Eli's ridiculous

expression nearly caused her to giggle. She lifted a hand to her mouth to cover her slight smile.

"Please, don't cover up such a beautiful face," he said. "It is the one perk of the assignment."

Perk? She could feel the warmth grow in her cheeks. "You speak with strange words, Elijah Miller."

"I've been gone a long time."

His lips curved with the hint of a smile. How handsome his face was to behold. She remembered how the sight of him had always stolen a little of her breath. She feared she would reveal too much if she said a single word. It was best to do as she had promised—to keep silent. This would all pass, even if there was a part of her that wanted to know the truth.

"You won't talk to me, then?" He rose from the table.

"I cannot."

"No. You choose not to talk. It isn't the same, Hannah." He lifted a small black mobile phone from his pocket. "I'm going to call the Lancaster police and report the shooting. They'll have to come out and file a report."

"No. Please. You're the police. Isn't that enough?"

"You can't have it both ways. Either you talk to me and tell me the truth or I call Chief McClendon." He held his little phone in the air, waiting for her decision.

Hannah dropped her head between her hands. She did not want to see Chief McClendon again. But to speak the truth to Elijah…that might be worse.

THREE

Eli walked onto the porch, frustrated and defeated—not so different than he had all those years ago when Hannah had refused him without so much as an explanation. Being back in Willow Trace was harder than he'd anticipated. He hadn't counted on all those old emotions resurfacing the second he laid eyes on her. Yet he knew he needed to be there no matter what he'd said to Hannah or how badly he'd like to go back to the city.

Hannah needed protection. Maybe the Amish had survived centuries with very little police or other government interference, but the governor had called him there. Clearly this situation was even more dangerous than Eli had suspected. Anyway, Elijah didn't believe in coincidence. He'd prayed for confirmation that his presence was needed there, and God had answered that in a big way. Jessica's death was no accident— even if Hannah wouldn't talk, he could tell that she didn't believe that. Nor was the shooting at her house a mere coincidence.

The sad truth, though, was that if he couldn't convince Hannah to talk to him, then there was no chance anyone else would. She had the most to gain by learning the truth, and there she was ordering him away—Hannah whom at one time he'd been so close to and shared all his dreams with. She saw him as an outsider now. It shouldn't upset him. He shouldn't take it so personally. He was just there to do a job. Right?

He watched through the window as back inside the house, Hannah went back to her broom and dustpan, cleaning the broken window up from the floors. What was she hiding? He had a wild impulse to hold her gently until she cried and told him all her secrets, to make her see that he was still the same person he'd always been.

Focus on the case, Miller. Do your job and get out of Willow Trace. Hannah had never been for him. How could he even think such a thing after the way she'd broken his heart and never looked back? His grip on the phone tightened. He turned his back to Hannah and dialed the private number given to him by Captain O'Dell.

"McClendon."

"Hello, sir. This is Detective Miller in Willow Trace, as per your request. Within five minutes of my arrival, there was a shooting incident—

someone firing from the woods toward the Nolts' home. No one is injured, but I thought—"

"I'll be right out." The line disconnected.

Not much of a conversation. Eli put the phone away in his pocket. Then again the whole situation was strange—so much secrecy? No media coverage? The governor involved? He hoped to have a nice chat with McClendon when he got there.

Maybe there was a political connection. But to the Amish? That was a stretch. Who could find a group of people more unconnected to the political world? They didn't even vote. A young widow and her teenaged daughter were not likely to be involved in anything that would snag the governor's attention.

Soft footfalls behind him made him turn. Hannah had joined him on the porch with a tall glass of lemonade. "Drink."

"Denki." He took the glass. They both smiled at his use of Pennsylvania Dutch language. He laughed. "I haven't said that in years and already twice today."

Her cheeks became a lovely color of pink. Her green eyes shone brighter. For a second, Eli felt like a sixteen-year-old boy again—that very same boy who would have leapt ten feet into the air after feeling the tingle of Hannah's fingers brush against his own as she passed him a glass of lemonade.

Tender emotions rushed through him. How he'd loved her all those years ago. Every woman since, he'd compared to her beauty and her kindness and her soul. None had been able to match up.

Get a grip, Miller.

He stepped back, trying to smile nonchalantly. Good grief. He was there to investigate, not to rekindle an old flame, especially an old flame with the woman who had dumped him. Once in a lifetime was enough for that.

Eli drank down the crisp, sweet mixture and returned the empty glass to her. *Keep your mind on the investigation.* "McClendon is on his way."

She frowned, clearly displeased with him, and his heart sank all over again. "You have changed, Elijah Miller. I thought you would understand and remember our ways. I thought you would respect them."

"I do respect *our* ways." He paused, a bit surprised at his choice of words. "But when the outside world comes to you, you have to respect it, too. You don't have to be in it, but you have to let someone help you protect yourself from this danger. Hannah, remember when I was six and my *Dat* took me into the city for the first time? I was abducted the second I stepped off the train."

"*Jah.* I remember that story. God brought you home safe to us again."

"Yes, but with the help of a police officer. Let's face it. If that cop hadn't fired his gun and shot the man holding me, then I would have been the one who'd died that day. Not the criminal. Someone wants to hurt you, Hannah, you and your family. They've already succeeded once. Please, let me help keep you safe," he pleaded. "Tell me what you know instead of cleverly avoiding every one of my questions."

She shot him a furtive glance as if she considered his words. Then she moved away from him. "It is not our way. As you must already know, it was decided that Jessica had a terrible accident."

"A terrible accident?" He shook his head in disbelief. "If one of those bullets had hit us earlier today, would that have been an accident, too?"

Hannah kept her eyes low, avoiding his face. "I don't know why anyone would be shooting at the house. But, in any case, the Nolts do not want the police involved. Thomas said so himself. You know how it is."

"I remember, Hannah." He remembered more than he liked. "And sometimes that is best—to move on. But if you are now in danger, then it's time to be proactive. You don't want to give the shooter a second chance."

She backed away.

"Don't you even want to know what happened to your daughter?" He reached for the crook of her arm. "Forget the *Ordnung* talk for one second and be straight with me."

She yanked her arm away.

Good. He was getting to her, even if he was pushing her in an uncomfortable way. She had to see that she needed to both accept God's will here and protect herself. And for that, he would push as hard as needed.

"You do, don't you?" he continued. "You do want to know what happened. The report said that you found her. Hannah, is that true? You found her in the barn at milking time? I saw the pictures. Tell me what happened that morning."

Hannah kept her eyes to the floor. Her jaw clenched.

"I can see you want to tell me something. Why don't you just say it?"

"I can't. I'm sorry, Eli. You should go home and leave us be."

A different question—what if he tried a different question? "Not until you talk to me. Where was Jessica before she died? Had she gone into the city? You know something, Hannah. I can see it in your face."

"You're wasting your time, Elijah. Jessica is gone and there's nothing to be done about it. Go back and tell your people that we do things differently here."

"I can't. McClendon is on his way. The governor asked me to be here. Please, Hannah." He stepped closer and spoke at a whisper. "Tell me what happened."

She looked up at him, tears glistening in her eyes. "I don't need to know what happened to Jessica. Without her, I don't even know if I care that I live. I have nothing left."

He swallowed hard. His heart ached for Hannah. More than ever he wanted to pull her the rest of the way into his arms and hold her tight. He wanted to let her release all of her pain and confusion. He wanted to remove her sweet prayer *Kapp,* run his hands through her locks of raven curls and remind her of how beautiful and precious she was. He wanted to press his lips to hers and kiss away her sorrow. But he knew she didn't want him to. Maybe she never did.

Elijah's firm grip on her arms gave Hannah a feeling of support she hadn't experienced in many years. His breath brushed warm and soft against her face. She should not let him hold her so close, but there was no strength in her to push him away. Her brain was befuddled as his questions swirled in her head while his touch both comforted and frightened her. She wanted to tell him everything—about Jessica, about Peter, about how she could never have children. But fear kept her mouth tight.

"*Hannah, gehts-du innen*—get into the *Haus*." Thomas's deep voice boomed across the porch.

Hannah and Elijah broke from their near embrace. She turned to face her brother-in-law where he stood at the edge of the porch carrying a large satchel of horse feed that made his muscles bulge. He looked as angry as she had ever seen him. "Thomas, brother, you remember your friend, Elijah Miller."

"I do." He gave a curt nod.

"He has come to pay his respects," Hannah explained.

"Actually, I'm here to investigate your niece's death," Elijah said. "I was trying to get Hannah to talk about the day you found Jessica. From the pictures of your niece postmortem, it looks very possible that she was murdered. Some of the police feel the matter should be looked into. Perhaps you can fill me in on things? Hannah doesn't feel she should talk to me."

"Looked to me like you were investigating something else." Thomas eyed Hannah. "I am certain Hannah explained our wishes in both matters."

"*Both* matters?" Elijah's confusion was apparent. Hannah shrank back toward the door of the cottage. She wanted to run into the house, but she knew that that would only make matters worse. How could Thomas bring up such a topic only a few days after Jessica's death? It was not unusual for a widow to marry the unwed brother of her deceased. But nothing had been decided, and they had not talked about such a union in months.

"Oh…oh…you—you are betrothed? No. Hannah didn't mention that." Elijah glanced back and forth between the two of them, then moved toward Thomas. "But no need to upset yourself, old friend. I'm here on business. Just after I arrived, shots were fired at the house. I think for your safety you should tell me what you know that could be relevant."

Thomas's look of anger softened quickly into concern as he turned to Hannah. "Is this true? Someone shot at you?"

She glared at Elijah, her mind full of his touch. How unaffected he seemed by the moment and the news that she was betrothed—even if it was false. She looked back to Thomas and tried to ignore the disappointment that weighed on her. "It is true, brother. You can see for yourself the broken window."

Thomas dropped his large pack and hopped up the steps. "But you are fine, no?"

"*Jah,* I am fine." She gathered her wits as best she could. "Mr. Miller has been kind enough to call your friend Chief McClendon. I believe he is expected soon, ain't so? I will finish cleaning the glass and make coffee."

Hannah scrambled inside the house, leaving the two men to puff their feathers for each other. She was mad at them both. She had never promised to marry Thomas, although he had asked her once and she had requested time to think on it. And Elijah should not have taken hold of her in such a bold way, grabbing on to all her senses the way he did.

That impulse she felt in that moment when she'd wanted to tell him everything…that was clearly just Elijah's bad influence at work. Thomas had made the decision that they would not seek answers as to what had happened to Jessica, and it was her duty to follow his wishes. Elijah had no business asking her to open her heart and share her thoughts and fears with him. He had shown their community that he could not be relied upon when he left them all behind, abandoning his family and breaking his father's heart.

At least now Thomas was home and he could tell Elijah to leave. He did not belong there. He was no longer one of them.

FOUR

Evening came fresh and cool. After a large helping of Hannah's hearty shepherd's pie, Eli followed Chief McClendon and Thomas Nolt onto the front porch.

He stopped at the edge of the stoop and looked into the clear night sky. He had forgotten how many stars one could see on a clear night in the country sky. He'd forgotten the rushing sounds of the wind, and of the leaves, and of the livestock milling about. Even the smells, he'd forgotten— that earthy blend of grasses and compost and animal and home cooking and unfinished wood.

It's true, Lord. Here, it is easier to see You, to hear You, to be with You. He breathed in deeply all the familiar odors and smiled up at the night sky. If only he could record all the sensations for when he returned home to the city.

The other men's voices pulled him back to the moment. Chief McClendon turned to Thomas.

"I thank your family for such kindness to me this evening."

"*Gut* to see you, Chief. Not so *gut,* your reason for coming." Thomas gave Eli a frosty glare. Then the two men shook hands like old pals, while Eli stood there, feeling about as welcomed as the Plague.

He had not expected a warm welcome from his old school friend and neighbor, but he hadn't expected one quite this glacial, either. He supposed it was his fault seeing as the man had caught Hannah practically in his arms. Even though Thomas and Hannah were not engaged, as Thomas had insinuated, Thomas's intentions seemed clear. At the very least it was readily apparent that he felt completely responsible for Hannah and very protective toward her. Hannah's feelings on the matter were less obvious. She attended to Thomas as head of the household, but she didn't show him any particular regard—not that Elijah was taking notes or anything. He couldn't have cared less. He had no interest in Hannah. He'd just been trying to get her to talk to him, and if Thomas hadn't shown up when he did, she would have. He was sure of it.

Eli glanced through the broken window at her, washing up dishes in the kitchen. She turned as if aware of him, offered a smile, then quickly averted her eyes back to her work.

Right. He felt nothing for her. The spike in his pulse must have been agitated nerves from his unexpected return to Willow Trace. Eli sighed and tried to focus once again on the case. "So, Hannah found the girl as I saw her in the pictures that you, Chief McClendon, took and filed away without further inquiry?"

McClendon shook his head, some regret in his expression. "I've been working with the Plain folk long enough to know what is acceptable. I do try not to interfere, but this case is different. I don't feel comfortable simply walking away. Thomas, consider making allowances this time."

"We appreciate Chief McClendon's respect. That is why Mr. Miller need not stay in Willow Trace," Thomas said.

McClendon frowned at Thomas. "As I said, I don't usually interfere, but I think this case is different. Call it instinct. I should have some of it after working the job for twenty-five years. Thomas, I hope you'll accept my advice to have Detective Miller stay on at the farm for a day or two. Losing *one* of you has been hard enough. And with the incident that occurred today, I cannot turn a blind eye."

Thomas and Eli looked uncomfortably at each other.

Eli had about as much desire to stay at the Nolts' as Thomas had for him to be his guest.

But from the way McClendon was behaving, it seemed as if the alternative was to have a patrol car on the farm, and neither McClendon nor Thomas would have any part of that. Eli tried to hide his skepticism. The Lancaster County Police Department was a large organization. It was hard to believe there wasn't one trustworthy individual among its ranks to work with the Amish. As far as Eli was concerned, McClendon, Hannah and Thomas were all hiding something, and he intended to find out what that was. How the governor fit into all of this he couldn't even imagine.

At dinner, he had not gleaned much new information. But one thing was certain—they all knew Jessica's death was no accident. There was an undercurrent of fear riding through the house.

Thomas frowned. "I made a mistake to leave Hannah alone at the house today. It will not happen again, I assure you both."

The chief nodded. "I know you'll make every effort to take care of your own. And normally, I wouldn't press my ways on you. But I'm asking you this one time to keep Mr. Miller close. He's got a phone and a radio and—"

"And a gun," Thomas finished his sentence.

"And a gun." The chief nodded and turned toward his car. "I'll check with you tomorrow, Detective." He stepped into his squad car and drove away.

Don't call us, we'll call you, Eli thought. *Thanks, Chief.* What was that? No explanation of the pictures. No mention of what had happened to the girl's clothing. No hint of a theory as to who had been behind the shooting earlier.

As the Lancaster chief drove away, the tension between Thomas and Elijah returned in full. They stood in silence on opposite ends of the porch.

"I didn't ask for this case," Eli said at length. "But now that it has been assigned to me, I intend to see it through."

"Meaning what exactly?" Thomas glared back at him.

"Meaning I'll be around for a few days asking questions about Jessica, about her friends and about her death."

"Questions to Hannah? Questions *about* Hannah?" Thomas folded his arms over his chest, making him seem even larger than he already was.

"I'll be asking questions of all of you." Eli shifted his weight. "It is what I do. Solve crimes. Find the bad guys. I don't want to be here any more than you want me here. So if you want to make my stay shorter, then tell me what happened to Jessica so I can do my job and get out of here."

"And what if there are not any bad guys, as you say?" Thomas said. "What if Jessica's death was an accident?"

"I find that a little hard to swallow after what happened this afternoon. I'm pretty sure you do, too. Look, I had planned to stay at the bed-and-breakfast. You're clearly uncomfortable with—"

"No." Thomas put his hand up stiffly. "It will not be said that I did not protect my family. Come. I will show you where you will stay tonight…in the horses' stable."

Hannah could not sleep. The sound of bullets zipped through her brain. The crash of glass breaking. The cold feel of Jessica's hands. The black car whizzing away from the barn.

And Elijah Miller. The warm touch of his hands on her elbow, that soft way he gazed at her—even after all these years. A softness she did not deserve. She'd broken his heart when she'd chosen Peter. Or so his sister, Abigail, had told her. And for what? To have a family with Peter and his daughter—a family she would lose before she turned thirty. Even though she was unable to birth children, she'd wanted so badly to be a mother. She couldn't have known how it would end. But not once had she regretted her choice in Peter. He had been a wonderful husband and *Dat* and friend.

She noticed, too, that Elijah seemed happy in his choice not to take vows. Still he had sat so comfortably at the dinner table among them—

despite the awkwardness with Thomas. He'd put his weapon away and eaten a king's portion of her cooking. That was most pleasing to her. He had talked freely about his work. And what work he did! She couldn't imagine the frightening things he faced in the outside world. She could never...

Under streams of white moonlight, Hannah stared through her small window down the path to where Eli slept in the horses' stable. Thomas was a bear for making him sleep out in the cold. Although the way Mama Ruth snored, Eli might find it a kindness not to be in the house with them.

What truly wasn't right was that Elijah still had not been told anything about Jessica's death and the black car. He was not stupid. He knew they weren't telling him everything. And while she did believe that God wanted them to accept what had happened to Jessica, she also believed that there could be good in discovering the truth—if it kept her safe, if it saved another from Jessica's fate. As Elijah had pointed out to her earlier, there was good in the work of the police. It was not merely to pass judgment and serve vengeance. They were there to protect, as well.

That's why tomorrow she would talk to Thomas and convince him to tell Elijah the whole story of the black car, the change of clothes, the blood-stains and the intruder in the barn.

Elijah, who after all these years still made her heart race. He'd grown even more handsome since she'd seen him last—stronger, taller. When he'd arrived at the front of the house, her heart had nearly flipped inside her chest. He'd looked so fine and fancy in the tight-collared shirt and jeans. And those huge blue eyes of his had always muddled her thoughts. What fun they had had together so long ago. How quick he had always been to make her smile.

The groan of wood bending sounded from the stairwell. Hannah sat up quickly and held in her breath. Someone was on the stairs. Who could it be? They'd all gone to bed hours ago.

She listened, but Ruth's snores filled the air again and there was nothing else to be heard. Maybe it was Thomas? He usually slept in *Dawdi Haus,* but he wasn't much of a sleeper. He could be up checking on things. And, really, who could sleep with all that snoring?

Hannah sighed and pulled the covers over her shoulders. Thomas was a good man and very protective of those he loved. She knew that he cared for her, as she did for him. He was sweet to offer her marriage. But something had kept her from giving him an answer to his proposal. Today, after seeing Eli Miller, she couldn't help wondering if her hesitation had something to do with racing pulses and easy smiles.

*Should that matter, Lord? Should the shivers
and chills a man gives us with a glance make a
difference to our hearts?*

She didn't know. Truth be told she'd forgotten all about those kinds of feelings. Until today.

*I must be the silliest woman on the earth to
wonder such things,* she scolded herself. *I know
what matters, Lord. That I serve You in all I say
and do.*

She doubted that included thoughts of Elijah
Miller and his blue jeans. *Goodness.* What had
gotten into her head? It wasn't as if she and Elijah could ever be together. He was an outsider.
She'd be shunned by the People—never allowed
to return, or have a meal with them, or pray, or
even speak with them. She would never even consider such a thing....

Anyway, Elijah Miller wasn't interested in her.
Ach! He'd shown nothing but disdain at being
back in Willow Trace. Her thoughts must be the
result of a tired mind.

It was late. She needed sleep. Without Jessica,
she had twice as much work to do around the
house. Hannah closed her eyes tight. But still
sleep did not come. In between the rhythmic crescendos of Nana Ruth's loud expirations, Hannah
heard the downstairs floorboards creak again.
She sat up again and fumbled on the nightstand

until she found her small candle and lit it. Should she go downstairs?

If Thomas wasn't sleeping either, she would go down now and talk to him. She slipped from bed, pulled one of her dark frocks over her head and hooked it quickly up her back. After tucking her long braid into a bun, she grabbed a bonnet that lay on the chest at the end of her bed. It was Jessica's, but it fit well enough. Then she blew out her candle and slipped down the stairs in bare feet.

"Thomas?" she whispered into the dark room. At the foot of the stairs, she searched the corners of the large room. A few beams of moonlight lit the space, as well as the dying embers in the fireplace. It must have been later than she thought. A shiver trickled down her spine. The hole in the window had left the room quite chilly. Thomas would have to get a new piece of glass for that right away.

Speaking of Thomas, where was he? The downstairs seemed to be empty. "Thomas? Are you there?"

Hannah shuffled to a chair in front of the fire where a nice warm quilt lay. She unfolded the heavy blanket and draped it over her shoulders.

Click.

Her head turned fast to the front door. It popped open and swung wide, letting in another blast of cool air.

"Thomas?" she called loudly this time. Still no answer. Had the door opened on its own? No. Thomas had locked it.

Hannah's pulse spiked as she had that feeling again—that feeling she'd had in the barn the other morning. The feeling she was not alone. Coming downstairs had been a bad idea.

She peered out onto the dark porch. "Thomas? Are you there?"

Another floorboard creaked; her heart plummeted. Thomas was not outside. But someone was there, in the kitchen. She had to get back upstairs and wake Nana Ruth. Forgetting the opened door, Hannah raced back over the hardwood floors to the bottom of the steps.

She looked up, ready to ascend, when she realized her mistake. The intruder was not in the kitchen. He was on the stairs.

A man dressed in all black came at her from the stairwell, face hidden in the shadows. He pushed her down to the floor, almost as if he had tripped. Her hands became pinned beneath her chest. Her head landed with a *thunk* onto the hardwood.

"Don't make a sound," he said. "I won't hurt you. I just... I need the journal. You have it. I know you do."

He came down on her, pressing a knee in her back so that she could not get free. "So, where is it?"

Where was what? What was he talking about? She knew nothing about a journal. "I have no journal," she pleaded. "I know not of what you speak."

He pushed her harder into the floor. "But you *have* to. You *have* to have Jessica's journal. She said you knew about it, about where it was. I need it. You need it. Where is it?"

Jessica's journal? What was he talking about? How could Jessica have a journal? Hannah and Nana Ruth had already been through the girl's things. There was nothing like a journal. She knew not what to say to this man. But she wondered if this journal he spoke of was the reason for Jessica's death.

Help me, Lord. What do I do?

FIVE

The trainer's quarters in the horse stable proved more accommodating than Eli had expected. But its location was lousy for keeping an eye on the main house. At midnight, instead of sleeping with the Nolts' prize-winning horses, Eli sat in his car with the motor running, watching the house and having a conversation with his partner, Mitchell Tucci.

"What do you mean you're working with another partner?" he asked his partner of five years.

"O'Dell assigned me to work with Sid Kaufman. Said you would be too busy to get back in time to wrap up the Mason-Hendricks case."

"But I shouldn't be here long at all. A couple of days tops. And we've been working on that case for months." Eli tried to control the sudden mixture of anger and fear that overwhelmed him—the feeling that he would never escape Willow Trace or have a job to return to when he did.

"So, what's the assignment?" Tucci asked. "O'Dell made it sound top secret, like FBI stuff."

"Top secret? In my hometown? Tucci, this is Willow Trace. The only thing top secret around here is Emily Matheson's recipe for apple pie."

"I thought you said bullets were flying as soon as you got there," Tucci reminded him. "Maybe it's more complicated than you think."

Eli slumped in the driver's seat. His partner was right even if he didn't want to admit it out loud.

"You think they were shooting at you and not at the old love of your life?" Tucci asked.

"Yeah, I thought about that angle. But it doesn't really add up. Only O'Dell knew I was here at that point. And consider that the shooter missed purposely and cleaned up his casings. If a professional were after me, he wouldn't have missed. Any of my enemies would just want me dead."

"Maybe a warning for you to get off the case?"

"But from whom? O'Dell? He just sent me here."

"Hey, man, I'm just looking at possibilities. Trying to help out. I thought you said the local chief suspects some strong anti-Amish sentiment in his ranks."

"Chief McClendon, yeah. He's hard to read. On the one hand, he seemed to really care about the safety of this family."

"And on the other hand?"

"And on the other hand, he's leaving everything up to me…and he doesn't even know me. I don't get it. In some ways, I feel like I'm being set up to fail and this is the one place on Earth where I absolutely cannot fail. That would just show my people that I was wrong to leave. I can't let that happen."

"What does it matter to you what they think if you know you did the right thing for you? You never worried about that before, did you?"

"Yeah. I guess. I don't know." Eli pushed the troubling thoughts away.

"Well, let me know if there's anything I can do to help out. Don't be a stranger."

Help. That was exactly what he needed. "Really? You wanna help me out?" Eli asked.

"Of course, I've always wanted to come out there and see where you're from."

"Oh." Eli paused. His loudmouthed Italian city slicker partner in Willow Trace was not exactly what he'd had in mind. "Actually, I wanted you to run some names and take some photos to the coroner."

Tucci laughed. "I can do that, too. Shoot me the names and pics."

"Names…well, anything on Jessica Nolt, Hannah Nolt, Thomas Nolt, Chief McClendon and Governor Derry. I'll email the photos."

The line went silent.

"Tucci? You copy?"

"I copy. The governor? You want me to run a check on Governor Derry? Where did that come from? And how? You know I don't have clearance for that."

"O'Dell said Derry asked for me on this case. But Governor Derry doesn't know me, so I want to know how he came about this idea. I think he must have some ties to the Willow Trace community, know what I mean? Anyway, maybe it would help if I knew what that connection was. I was thinking you could call that friend of yours at the bureau. He owes us a favor, right?"

"That he does." Tucci chuckled.

"And don't check everything. Just connections to Willow Trace or the Lancaster police. Maybe you won't get anything, but it's worth a try. Got to start somewhere."

"I hear you. Wow. The governor asked for you? This is making the Mason-Hendricks case look pretty lame. You sure you don't need me to come out there? Shake things up a little?"

"Maybe later," Eli said. "I'll send the pics through my phone as soon as we hang up."

"I'm off to run the names," Tucci said, and ended the call.

Eli clicked off. He missed his friend and he found it disturbing that O'Dell had replaced him on the Mason-Hendricks case. But he could hardly worry about that now.

From his lap, he lifted the small file folder created by the Lancaster police concerning Jessica Nolt's death. He hadn't had a chance to review it since leaving his office.

Eli flipped through the folder reading the pages with a penlight. There wasn't much there. Only pictures and the information on the family. With his cell phone, he took photos of each image and then emailed them to his partner with a message. Run these by Michelle at the coroner's office. Tell me what she sees.

If Tucci could get anything from Michelle, it would be helpful, as he did not even know the probable cause or time of death. Never before had he worked a case with so little to go on.

Tomorrow, he needed to talk to Jessica's friends. He'd get a list of them from Hannah. Perhaps she could also show him how and where she found the body. Although with Thomas hanging around, he feared it would be difficult to get her to open up.

Eli tossed the file folder into the passenger seat and leaned back, struggling to get comfortable in his small car. His phone battery was still low. Might as well keep the engine running and let it charge for a few. Wasn't as if there were a lot of electrical outlets where he could plug in for the night. He needed to shut his eyes for a few minutes. It had been a long day and tomorrow would probably be longer. The more time he spent in Willow Trace, the bigger chance of his having to confront his own family. It was certain by now, with the help of Nicholas, they knew of his return.

He squirmed, still trying to get comfortable, his eyes focusing on the upstairs window of the cottage, where a dim light appeared behind the green curtain. It was the window he guessed to belong to Hannah's bedroom, as per his estimation from running through the house earlier that afternoon. The Amish had no fancy closets but hung their clothing on pegs. He was pretty certain he'd distinguished between Hannah's frocks and those of the slightly larger Nana Ruth. But why a light in Hannah's room at this hour? It was late. What could she be doing awake? She must be exhausted. But perhaps she was troubled after the scare she'd had that afternoon. That could not have been easy. Poor Hannah. She had lost so much. Although part of him was angry with her, as it was clear she knew more than she was telling him, he couldn't help empathizing with her pain. He glanced again at the photos of her daughter. How horrible it must have been to find her.

Faint shadows fluttered behind the dark green shade of Hannah's room. Maybe she and Thomas were talking. His body tensed at that thought. Or was that his gut telling him that something was wrong up at the house? As if he would know. Seemed his instincts had gone on holiday the minute he saw Hannah. His head was a mess. He should probably be doing more than sitting in his car.

Eli killed the engine and rolled down the window. It was a stretch to think he could hear anything at that distance, but certainly he could hear more with the window down than up. Having one person in the house killed and another shot at, there was no such thing as being too careful.

His cell phone vibrated in the seat beside him. He checked the screen. Tucci.

"That was fast," Eli answered the call. "Did you get my pictures?"

"I did. I'll send those to Michelle in the morning," Tucci said. "Got something else, too."

"What's that?" Eli tried to focus on the conversation with Tucci, but the flickering light inside Hannah's room was extinguished. He sat up straight, his senses on full alert.

"My friend Jim at the FBI was up late and ran your names."

"And he found something that fast?"

"Yep, it may be nothing but I thought I'd pass it on."

"Please."

"So, apparently there was one prize-winning

cross-draft pony stallion sold about six months ago by a T. Nolt to our very own Governor Derry for the sum of eighty-six thousand dollars." Tucci emphasized the price of the sale.

"Whoa. A pony for that kind of money? And to Governor Derry?"

"Paid in cash, too. I thought you might—"

"Shh." Eli shushed his friend. The faint sounds of a distant shriek reached his ears. "Did you hear that?"

"Hear what?"

Eli's heart began to pound. Had that been Hannah? "You didn't hear anything?" he whispered into the phone.

"Nothing," Tucci said.

Eli listened but the night had fallen quiet again. "Uh...I don't know. Probably a cat, but I'm going to run a perimeter check on the house and barns. Keep digging, Mitchie. I'll call you in the morning."

Eli was already sliding out of the car, grabbing his flashlight and pocketing his phone, before his partner could respond. Eli didn't really believe he'd heard a cat. That was a woman's scream. And he believed it was Hannah's. Thomas might not want him to, but he was going back inside the house.

Without a sound, he closed the door to his car. Then slinking his way under the tree-covered path, he dashed toward the house. Another muffled cry broke through the night. This one louder than the first and confirming his hunch. It *was* Hannah. She was in trouble.

Glock drawn, Eli sneaked to the porch, sucking in a gasp when he saw that the front door to the cottage hung wide open. From the bottom of the steps, he could hear a muffled voice inside speaking fast and low.

Eli clenched his teeth, resisting the temptation to bust into the house and attack whoever was making Hannah scream. Of course, he knew that would be dumb. It was too dark and the downstairs was too large and open. If he raced inside, he'd be nothing more than an easy target standing in the doorway with a flashlight to help the bad guy aim better.

Instead, Eli tucked the flashlight into his belt and lowered himself into a squatting position. He could creep up the front stairs and slink into the house slowly, unnoticed. That way he could get a better handle on the situation. But as he pressed his weight over the first step, it groaned loudly under him.

Stupid old house. Heavy footsteps scrambled across the floor inside. The intruder was getting away. Again.

Eli leaped like a cat through the front door, aiming both his gun and flashlight in the direction of the footsteps. Target or not, he wanted a chance at this guy. At the other end of the kitchen, he caught the backside of him. A man in all black. Thin. Tall. Quick.

"Hold it. Freeze. Philadelphia police." Eli cocked his gun and aimed for the man's heart.

SIX

The dark figure in the kitchen door did not stop as Eli commanded but continued straight through the opened screen and out into the darkness. Eli knew he should chase after him, but a more pressing concern came first.

"Hannah!" Eli moved across the room, the beam from his flashlight finding her lying face-down near the bottom of the stairs. "It's me, Eli. Are you okay?"

He knelt beside her. Putting a hand to her shoulder, he could feel her shaking.

"So glad that you are come." Her voice quivered as he unraveled her from the quilt that seemed to have her trapped to the floor. Her prayer *Kapp* had slipped from her hair, her apron unpinned; her face was red, splotchy and swollen.

"Can you move?"

"I think so."

Eli helped her to a seated position. "Are you going to be okay?"

She gestured to the back door. "Yes. Go. Go after him."

Elijah took off through the back and searched for the fleeing intruder. All was dark. The backyard and garden were empty. But as he turned to go back inside, his eye caught a flicker of movement in the distance. There, in the distance, he could barely make out the silhouette of a man. He seemed to move his arms rapidly through the air over and across something large and dark. For a second, Eli feared the man had a weapon, but when a second later his figure lifted high from the ground. Eli realized he'd mounted a horse and was already galloping away into the night.

Eli turned and went back into the house.

Who was that? Who pushed me down? Had she known his voice or had she just imagined that? Hannah pushed herself up from the hardwood floor and turned on the oil-powered overhead light. An agonizing pain stabbed through her head, followed by a steady rhythmic throbbing, making her want to tear her hair out by the roots and vomit. She stumbled her way to the small couch by the woodstove and carefully sat back into the cushions. The movement filled her with nausea and she doubled over her lap, hoping to swallow away a dry heave.

Eli stepped back through the back door. Slowly, she turned her aching head toward him.

"Whoever it was rode off on a horse." He shrugged. "Only in Willow Trace, right?"

No black car, she thought. But someone on horseback, that brought things a little too close to home. "What kind of horse?" she asked.

"Uh…black? But don't they all look black in the dark?"

"No." She looked away from his attempt to make her smile. How had that almost worked? Two minutes ago she'd been scared out of her mind. His presence had such an effect on her. It should not be so.

"Where are Thomas and Nana?" he asked.

"I can hear Nana still sleeping," she said. "I don't…I don't know about Thomas. He's not usually a heavy sleeper."

Eli nodded thoughtfully, then moved toward her, slowly taking the seat next to her. He reached for her hands and covered them over with his own. *Thomas.* She hadn't even thought of him since the attacker confronted her. When she'd been afraid, it had been Elijah she'd wanted and welcomed. Her hands felt warm and safe inside his. She should have been ashamed, the feelings he stirred in her. She should have pulled away. He was not her beau. He was not one of their community anymore. And yet his eyes held her in a tender gaze from which she could not look away.

"You need a doctor," he said.

She felt her eyes widen. "No. No doctor. I'm fine."

Eli looked doubtful.

"That is, I'll be fine," she amended.

"Then tell me what happened tonight," he whispered.

No. She closed her eyes tight. She didn't want to remember. But her mind rushed back to the hard push to the floor. Tears flooded her eyes and crashed down her cheeks. She looked away, pulled her hands back and turned from him. "What if you had not come when you did? I—I am so thankful to God—"

"Me, too." His voice was soft, reassuring. "Glad I wasn't in the stable or I would never have seen your light on and heard you scream."

She nodded and slowly opened her eyes to him again. How the strength and softness in him blended and touched her through his deep gaze. He reached up and wiped away the moisture from her cheek. "I know you don't feel well, but…can you tell me what happened? It's best with victims if they talk about things right away."

Victim? Was that what she was? It was hard to put such a title to herself, to think she was different from anyone else. Special. The idea conflicted her. She took in a deep, shaky breath and wiped away the rest of her tears.

"Tell me what happened, Hannah. I need to know about everything."

"Everything?" Her gaze went down to the wooden floor. "I—I wouldn't know where to begin with everything. I feel so confused inside since—"

"Then start with tonight. You turned on a light, didn't you?"

She nodded.

"Start there."

"I could not sleep. My mind was racing with thoughts of…" Hannah pressed her lips together. Her thoughts had been on Eli and all that he made her feel inside. But she would not speak of that. He must never know she still loved him. Had always loved him. If it had not been for Jessica…

"Your mind was racing. Mine, too." He smiled and patted her shoulder sweetly.

"*Jah.* So, I am awake and I think I hear someone moving downstairs. I think it must be Thomas. I dress and come down to talk because I have things to say about…" How did she keep getting back to Elijah?

"But it wasn't Thomas." Elijah tried to help her refocus.

"No. It was not Thomas. I realized that right away, but I see the front door is opened, so I go to close it. Then I hear someone moving. Oh, Elijah, I was so scared. I run to the steps, but…he got to me first. I was so frightened."

"I know. I know. But you are safe now." He put a gentle arm around her shoulders and pulled her close to his side. "You're safe. Relax."

Hannah could not tell if she stiffened from his touch or melted into his arms. There was such a mixture of emotions inside her. For certain, her heart beat faster and her breath shortened. But it was no longer from fear that her body reacted, but from Elijah's scent and touch and kindness to her.

"What happened next? You were near the stairs when I got here."

"*Jah,* so I run for the stairs but he pushes me down and asks me for… he asks for…for something. I don't remember."

"Did you see his face?"

"No. It was too dark. Pushed me to the floor. Very strong."

"Yes, you have a nasty bump on your forehead. How about we get some ice on that? You should put your feet up, too."

Eli propped her feet on the table in front of the couch then left her to fetch a few ice cubes from the oil-powered freezer. He wrapped some ice in a dish towel and returned to her side, placing the homemade cold pack on her head.

"Aye." She backed away from his hand. "It

must be more than a bump." She reached for the ice bundle and took it from his fingers.

"It's quite a knot." He smiled and sat down again. "I should call my sister and have her take a look at you."

"No. Thank you. I'm sure I'll be fine." Hannah located the giant bump on her head with one hand, then gently placed the ice around but not directly on the sore.

"Okay, but I'm going to stay here and keep an eye on you for a while. It's a nasty bump."

Hannah smiled at his concern, knowing she wanted him to stay for more than just to see about her health—his presence gave her a comfort she longed for.

"Can you remember anything else?" he asked. "I heard his voice when I got up to the house. Seemed he was saying quite a bit."

Hannah thought hard. "He did. He spoke like he was nervous. He mentioned Jessica. It was…it was almost like he knew me. And I knew him."

"What do you mean? Like he was Amish? Or someone from town?"

"I—I don't know." She closed her eyes, but her mind was blank. "I only remember thinking that there was something familiar about his voice. That is all. I am so sorry, Elijah. I wish I could keep it all straight in my head." She looked up again into his soft blue eyes. Why was it she could not remember five minutes ago while old forgotten feelings seemed so completely alive to her? Maybe Eli was right and she should have his sister look at her head. "We should inform Thomas of what has happened. He will not be pleased."

Eli didn't look so pleased, either. "Yeah. Okay. I'll go and wake him."

Hannah closed her eyes as he moved away. Her head pounded. "I'm sorry I cannot remember."

"It's okay, Hannah. It's been a long day. And you're doing as well as can be expected. Just relax and let the details come back na…"

Hannah opened her eyes when Elijah stopped midsentence. When she looked up, he was standing at the bottom of the stairs staring downward with a strange expression. "What is it?" she asked.

"The bottom step. It's been opened. You know, the storage area under the stairs. Did you keep anything in it?"

"Opened?" Hannah swallowed hard. Panic flashed through her as she remembered her attacker reaching over her toward the step. "Yes… or at least Thomas used to keep some things there. Why?"

Eli turned back, shaking his head. "Because it's empty. What was in it?"

"I am not sure. Maybe nothing. Perhaps Thomas or Nana Ruth keeps something there, but I do not think so." The intruder had asked her for a journal, for Jessica's journal. What had the poor girl done? Gotten herself into? Hannah could not imagine. The room seemed to spin like the confusion in her head. Her chest tightened. The lump on her head ached.

"What is it, Hannah? Tell me."

Hannah could hardly hear Elijah's words over the noise in her own mind. She began to shake, her thoughts jumbled. In her head, voices, noises. The intruder. Jessica. Thomas. Elijah. Chief McClendon.

If only she had been a better mother to Jessica. None of this would be happening. "I should never have tried to be Jessica's mother. God did not want me to have children. I should have understood that. I should have—"

Eli stood before her. His warm hand touched her cheek. Hannah opened her eyes. He lifted her chin tenderly. "You were a wonderful mother, Hannah. I don't know what is happening here, but I am certain that it is not the result of your parenting skills."

Tears spilled from her eyes. How many people she had hurt in her own selfishness. How Elijah could be so kind to her after she had refused him she did not know. She grabbed his hand and the wrist and pressed her face against his warm palm. "You are gracious."

"No. Hannah, I'm not. But I can put the past in

the past. And I can assure you that you are in no way responsible for the things happening here."

Tears flushed from her eyes. He did not understand. Perhaps it was better that way. Perhaps he should never know the truth about why she had refused him, about how she had never stopped loving him, about how feeling his warm touch against her cheek brought her more comfort and pleasure than he would ever know.

He drew back. "I know there is more that you have to tell me. I can see it in your eyes, but you're tired. I'm tired." He smiled. "Let's continue this in the morning. I'll go and tell Thomas what's happened. Stay here. I'll be back to help you up the stairs."

Hannah nodded in agreement. She *was* ready to tell him everything about Jessica, whether Thomas agreed to it or not.

Screech! The back door swung open.

Hannah squealed. Someone was there. Someone tall and dark and hidden in the darkness of the kitchen.

Elijah stepped forward, pulling his Glock from his waist. She turned her head away, not wanting to hear the gunfire. Nor see death. She had seen enough of that for a lifetime.

SEVEN

"I take it you did not expect me back so soon."

Eli relaxed his defensive stance. The man at the door was Thomas, dirty, disheveled and wet with sweat. Eli couldn't help picturing him as the man he'd seen mounting the horse and riding off in the night. Anger tightened Eli's fist around the butt of his gun as he put it away.

"Expect you back? We didn't know you had gone anywhere," he said. "At least now I understand why you didn't hear Hannah scream for help. You weren't here. Are you crazy leaving her after what happened this afternoon?"

Thomas's angry expression dropped. He came farther into the kitchen, his eyes wide. "But was it not you who sent me to go to Hostetlers' farm?"

"Me?" Eli laughed. "Why would I do such a thing?"

"I—I…."

"I'm not the enemy here, Thomas, and the sooner you figure that out, the safer we're all going to be." Eli clenched his teeth. His hands rolled into fists. "Hannah was attacked. Good thing I wasn't asleep in the stable or I would never have heard her scream."

"This is true?" Thomas looked worried now.

"Yes, Thomas. There was an intruder. I—" Hannah tried to stand, but not having the strength wobbled off balance.

Eli reached an arm to steady her. Thomas, having the same idea, moved forward as well, but stopped, as he was not needed.

"You are not well, Hannah. Allow me to fetch Abigail Miller or Dr. Peters for you," he said.

"No, brother. Truly, I am fine. Just a bump on the head." She pulled away from Elijah and made her way to the stairs.

"Would you not tell me what has happened?" Thomas asked.

"There will be time to talk tomorrow. I am tired."

"Good night, Hannah." Elijah smiled at her brave front. He knew inside she was hurt and very scared. He wanted to help her to her room, tuck her into her bed and kiss her soft cheek. He wanted to let her know he would keep her safe… if he could.

Thomas turned to Elijah. "Forgive me. I'd found a note at the front door saying that there was an ill foal at the Hostetlers' farm and that they requested my help. It is not unusual for a neighbor to ask such a thing, but when I got there and saw there was no trouble I rushed back and found you two together. I...I—"

"Do you have this note?" Eli asked. "Could I see it?"

Thomas produced a small white sheet of paper from his sleeve. The message was just as he'd said, written in carefully scripted block letters. Elijah studied it then handed it back to Thomas. "Hold on to this. I doubt it will be of use, though, as the script looks stilted. Probably anyone could have penned it. Although if it were the intruder... Hannah did say she thought she knew his voice. Did any neighbors know what you kept in the bottom stair?"

Thomas blanched and turned toward the staircase. A deep frown forced creases around his eyes. "This is...this is most disappointing."

"What *did* you keep there?" Eli hated to pry. It was not the Amish way, but he needed to know. He needed Thomas and Hannah to tell him the truth. He regretted that Thomas had cut his time with Hannah short. He sensed that finally she had been ready to tell him more about Jessica and the events leading up to her death. Hopefully, tomorrow he would get another chance.

"Cash." Thomas lifted up the step and examined the empty hole. He turned back, looking even more ill than before. "A lot of cash. I made some good trades recently. I was saving for..." He removed his hat and shook his head. "Oh, what does it matter? *The Lord giveth and the Lord taketh away.*"

"God didn't take your money, Thomas. A man did. A man that wore dark clothing and rode off on a horse. Was there anything else in there?"

Thomas nodded. "Some documents concerning the horses and a journal I keep on all their breeding and trades."

"Your trades?" Eli repeated, thinking of Thomas's high-dollar horse recently sold to the governor. "How involved was Jessica in your trading and training?"

"Not at all, really. Jessica was here in the house with Hannah, learning to cook and sew and garden. She fed and groomed the horses from time to time but nothing more and not much of that since she started courting."

"Jessica had a beau?"

"Daniel Hostetler, of course. They've been inseparable since they were children. It was no surprise to us that they began courting last year."

"And he is a large boy? Full grown?"

Thomas looked away. "I will not accuse my own brethren, nor help you to do so."

Elijah ground his teeth in frustration. What were they all hiding? And how was he ever to figure any of this out if they didn't help him instead of keeping secrets? "I'll need to talk to Daniel and any other friends of Jessica's first thing in the morning."

"If you must."

"I must...." Eli sighed heavily. "I'd like to see where you found Jessica's body, as well."

"Why? She is no longer there."

"Of course not, but I can imagine the scene as it was and try to piece together in my mind the events of that night she died."

"It is not our way to wonder about what has happened."

"No. But it's mine and I've been asked to look into it. Anything you can tell me about Jessica or anything unusual around here would be helpful."

"I can't imagine I know anything that would make a difference."

"How about your horse trade with Governor Derry?"

Thomas's face twitched. "Yes. A pony for his daughter and a good sale it was. But it has nothing to do with us now." He walked over and put a hand on Elijah's shoulder. "I am thankful you have helped Hannah this day. She is in a fragile state. But you will not take advantage of that to pry into things that are none of your concern— or to get any closer to Hannah than is proper. In any case, now that I think on it, I can keep a better eye on you if you stay here in the house." He gave a quick laugh. "Come now. We must get to bed. All this talk leads us to nothing."

"Did you want me to call McClendon about your break-in and the money that was stolen?"

"You see what good calling the police has brought us so far. No. And no more talk of it. Come. I'll show you to the spare room."

Eli locked the doors both front and back, something the Amish rarely did, and followed Thomas into the *Dawdi Haus* and up to the extra bedroom, too tired to think over all that needed sorting out. In particular, Mr. Daniel Hostetler.

Morning came all too quickly and Hannah rose, reminded of the lump on her forehead as standing brought a wave of pain to her head. At least the swelling had reduced during the night, she decided as she ran a cold, damp cloth over her face. A little headache never hurt anyone. She would be brave and face the day no matter how much she'd like to crawl back into her warm bed. There were still things to be happy about. She missed Jessica terribly, but she was in heaven now and at peace. Life on Earth moved on. She would move with it and her God would be enough. He would get her through this just as she had gotten through losing Peter. Oh, how thankful she was that He had already saved her from saying too much to Elijah last night. She must take care to guard herself better. He was not for her and she was not for him. Baring her soul to him would only make things harder when he left. And he would leave. That she was sure of. Just as he had left before.

Hannah dressed, taking great care when she pinned on her prayer *Kapp,* then went down and began breakfast. Nana Ruth came behind her and then Thomas, who looked as if he had not slept at all.

"You should fetch Elijah from the stable," Nana Ruth suggested to Thomas. "I am sure he will not be used to waking at this hour."

"I don't think Elijah Miller will be joining us for breakfast," Thomas said. Hannah nearly dropped the pan from her hands. What did he mean by that? Had Elijah left? Had Thomas sent him away?

She cracked an egg and dropped it into the hot skillet. It sizzled and popped and the room filled with its rich aroma of butter and breakfast. "Nana Ruth, would you watch over this egg while I fetch more from the henhouse? I'm afraid we're down to the last three."

Nana Ruth smiled. "I will go and fetch them myself," she said, taking the basket. "My old bones need a shake this morning."

She left through the back door.

Hannah fixed Thomas his plate and brought it to the table.

"How's your head?" he asked.

"Better." She stood back as Thomas prayed over his food. "Did he leave?"

Thomas took a bite of his breakfast and mumbled something inaudible. "It would be best that he would go back to the city. He's brought nothing but trouble here." He studied her. "Be careful, Hannah. He is not the boy you once knew."

"I do not know what you mean."

"I see how you look at him."

"I give him no better treatment than I would any guest in your home."

"Is it not your home, too?" He gazed into her eyes.

Hannah looked down. "I—I do not know. Now that Jessica is gone you do not need me here. I have no one to teach the sewing and cooking to. Nana is in good health. You can care for yourself. You did not even tell me that you were leaving the house last night. I thought…"

"We could marry this November, Hannah. Everyone expects it. That would give you the security you want."

"You cannot ask me to think on marriage so close to Jessica's death. I cannot." She hurried to the stove, embarrassed she had revealed her fears to him. Her question sounded like a push for him to renew his offer of marriage. And it was not. How could she think of marriage to him when her head was full of nothing but Elijah?

"Elijah showed you the bottom step? I told him I didn't think you kept anything in it," she said.

"There was the money there, Hannah."

"I'm sorry. I did not know."

"I have always kept a bit of cash on hand for emergencies. I am not troubled by its loss. It is nothing. The money was not mine. It belonged to God. I'm sure He knows where it is. I am only thankful you are safe."

Hannah looked back at him. "What if all of these events are related?"

"How do you mean? The money and Jessica? Were you listening to our conversation last night?"

"I was not."

"Did Elijah suggest this idea to you?"

Hannah began to feel angry with Thomas. He was being obtuse because of his jealousy. "He did not. I am perfectly capable of having the thought all by myself, I assure you. It makes sense. The man last night asked for a journal—he said it belonged to Jessica. He must have thought that he might find it there in the step."

"A journal? Did Jessica keep a journal?"

"I do not believe so. But I obviously knew very little about Jessica."

"Perhaps you are right. The events are related

somehow. There *was* a journal in the step—my journal, listing my trades. That must have been what was meant by the man's demands. And now that this person has our money and journal, there can be nothing left for anyone to come for. We are safe."

"You have already sent Eli home, haven't you?" Hannah turned back to the stove, her heart sinking. "I think your decision is unwise."

"You may think what you like. But I believe the intruder got what he wanted. There was a lot of money there, Hannah. That is what he wanted. Nothing more. And this is what we will report to the bishop and to Mother. There is enough talk amongst the people already because of Jessica's accident. This will end it.... Fix yourself some breakfast and trouble yourself no more over this."

Hannah began to fix a plate of fried eggs even though she wasn't hungry in the least. In fact, Thomas's talk of marriage had made her nearly ill. "But this man said he wanted *Jessica's* journal. Not yours. And not money. He was quite serious. He may have taken your money, but he will come back when he sees your journal is not the one that he wanted."

"He was after the money, Hannah. That is always what they want. He will not come back. You are safe now."

Hannah wanted to scream out her frustration,

but the arrival of a horse and buggy in front of the house put an end to the conversation.

Hannah glanced through the kitchen window. A woman dressed in a maroon frock and white apron descended the vehicle.

"Is Nana expecting a visitor?" she said.

Thomas shrugged. A light rap sounded at the front door. Hannah moved quickly to open the latch.

"*Guten Morgan,* Hannah Nolt. *Wie gehts?*" Abigail Miller looked as bright and cheerful as the morning sun itself. Her peppy voice washed through the room and Hannah allowed herself to smile for the first time that day.

"Come in, Miss Miller. Please. How nice to see you." Hannah opened the door wider so that Elijah's younger sister could enter.

"I have come to see my brother. He is here, ain't so?" She was nearly giddy with excitement.

"He is," Hannah said. "Or at least he was last night. I have not seen him this morning."

Thomas grumbled from the kitchen. Hannah felt her cheeks heat up. Abigail continued to smile, seemingly oblivious of the tension in the room until she moved closer to take a look at the lump on Hannah's forehead. "Oh dear, Hannah, your head. What has happened?"

"I'm afraid it looks much worse than it is." Hannah backed away. All she needed was one more person asking questions. "Thomas, could you tell Elijah that he has a visitor?"

"So he is still sleeping, is he?" Abigail smiled.

"Nope, I'm right here." Elijah stepped into the kitchen. His eyes fell softly on her. Hannah tried hard to be indifferent at the sight of him. Not that he cared or would have noticed the thrill he gave her. All too quickly, he looked away to his sister, grinning like a child with a new puppy.

Thomas stood from the table, took his hat from its peg on the wall and backed up to the kitchen door. "If you'll excuse me, I have work to do. Enjoy your morning. I'll return in time to head to the Millers' for the harvest this afternoon. Good day."

What? A harvest gathering at his family's place? That was exactly what Eli had hoped to avoid. Although seeing his sister there so happy to see him gave him great joy.

"Abby." He came forward and gave her a hug.

"You are just as I imagined," she teased.

"I hope not." He brushed a hand through his bed-head hair and made a wide-eyed face. For certain, he needed a few more hours' sleep and a shave. The Amish might not talk about outward appearances, but one as bad as his could hardly escape their notice. "You look well yourself, Abigail. So glad you're here. How is everyone? *Mamm?* Elizabeth?" He looked down before adding, *"Dat?"*

"Come see for yourself? I came just so. To invite you to cousin John's. Today we pick his strawberries. He has so many this year he decided to have a gathering to bring them in. I'll give you a ride myself if you like."

Eli shook his head. "No way. That is a terrible idea and you know it."

"And why is it a terrible idea?" Hannah asked. "I'm sure all of your family would like to see you."

"You're wrong about that. *Dat* said he never wanted to see me again, and unless I hear otherwise I'm not going to face him. It will be a disaster."

"Oh, come, now, Elijah. You are overreacting." Abigail gave him a disapproving glare.

"Am I?" Elijah frowned and tried not to resent the way his sister reminded him that he alone was the outcast child. How was it that Abigail had not yet joined the church and still lived among the People when he so much as mentioned the police academy and was instantly disowned? "I don't think so."

Hannah came back to the table with a cup of coffee for each of them. She served them and stood back from the table. "You should go, Elijah. Many will be there and among them most of Jessica's friends. You could ask them about the night before she died…if they had seen her, where they had been."

"So that is why you have come home?" Abigail was wide-eyed. "To ask questions about poor Jessica?"

"Yes," he answered, thinking over Hannah's words. It was true. He needed to talk to the community, especially Jessica's friends. But seeing his family was a bad idea. Not to mention that it would be hard to protect Hannah there. "No, I'm not going and neither are you, Hannah. It could be dangerous for you to be out in the open all day like that."

"Why would Hannah be in danger?" Abigail asked, looking confused. "What harm could come to her from a simple gathering?"

"It is of no consequence," Hannah replied.

Elijah frowned. This pattern of secrecy was going too far, making her actively ignore the danger she was in. But he wouldn't embarrass Hannah by arguing with her in front of a guest.

"What if I could promise you that *Dat* will not be there?" Abigail said teasingly.

"Yeah, right. Bishop Miller miss an opportunity to eat? I don't think so."

"No. I'm serious. It's the main reason I thought I'd come by and ask you to join us. *Dat* was called away to meet with the bishop from Grenlicht today. That's a long buggy ride even on a good day. He'll be gone for hours," his sister said.

"I don't know. It could still be dangerous…but I do need to talk to her friends."

"Exactly. Then it's settled. I'll be back at noon to pick you up." Abigail gave his cheek a kiss and headed back out.

Elijah watched her off, then turned, crossed his arms over his chest and glared at Hannah. "So, I guess now would be a good time for you to tell me about this journal of Jessica's? And about everything else you've been keeping from me."

EIGHT

"Father, we are thankful for what we are about to receive...."

Elijah's cousin John Miller stood at the head of the long table leading the blessing and giving thanks for his fine harvest of strawberries, which the entire community had come together to gather, sort and place in baskets to sell at market.

John was a plain man—the ideal Amish man, so to speak. His dirty-blond hair was cut in a simple bowl shape around his head. It fell slightly below the brim of his straw hat. His shirt was a loose-fitted button-up, the color of the sky. His trousers, black—no pockets, no zippers, no cuffs. His reddish-blond beard framed the outside of his chin and was trimmed away from his mouth and upper lip. It was a style belonging uniquely to the Amish.

If Elijah had stayed in Willow Trace instead of leaving when he turned eighteen, he guessed, he'd look much the same as his cousin. He certainly wouldn't be wearing a fitted pair of Levi's jeans and a golf shirt. His hair would be longer like John's and his face smooth, unless of course, he'd married....

A dry lump formed in his throat. He looked to Hannah. Marriage. He had wanted that with her so many years ago. He had wanted a family with her. He remembered how they'd talked about having three or four children. They had even decided on names. How was it that she changed her mind so suddenly?

Oh, what did he care anyway? He didn't. He could never come back to Willow Trace. Nor did he want to. If only Nana Ruth hadn't walked into the house the very second he'd asked Hannah about the journal, maybe he'd already be on his way back to the city.

Elijah knew he was trying to push away the pleasant experiences of home that had filled his senses all afternoon—the buggy ride, which he'd given in to despite his better judgment that they go in the car; working alongside his kinsmen and friends in the fields, the fine meal they took together, the sight of all the children dressed like miniature grown-ups running barefoot through the fields, playing tag and hide-and-seek and swinging from the same tire swing he had played in as a child. The sights had quite overwhelmed him.

And as his cousin prayed, full of grateful thanks

to both God and his family and friends, Elijah was moved to tears. He had forgotten the sense of community and traditions of his People. He'd forgotten his sense of belonging. He looked to his sister's wagon and remembered his gun and badge hidden under the blanket. What was wrong with him? Sure, it was great to be home for a few days, but he did not regret his choice to become a police officer. Nor was he ashamed of it. In fact, it was time to get back on the job and start asking around about Jessica.

After the meal, Eli zoned in on a group of young teens that sat on John's front porch, enjoying the evening breeze. He did not recognize their faces, as they would have been babies when he left town, but they would know him. Of that, he was certain. He hoped that would work to his advantage.

"Were any of you friends with Jessica Nolt?"

The group fell silent.

"You can talk to me. I'm Elijah Miller," he said. "I'm sure you knew me when you were little. I've just been gone awhile."

"You're the cop," one boy said.

Elijah neared them. He made the courteous gesture like tipping a hat, even though he wore none. "That's right. I'm the bishop's son that became a cop."

"Are you moving back here?" another child asked, turning a nice shade of red.

"No, just visiting." He looked around at the beautiful land. In the distance, Hannah was cleaning one of the dinner tables. Near to them, his mother, Nana Ruth and a few other women sat chatting in a small circle. His chest tightened at the sight. "Just visiting," he repeated as if to drive home his answer.

"Do you kill bad people?" a boy in the group asked.

"No. I've never had to kill anyone," he answered.

"Would you?" the boy continued. "My dad says guns are bad."

"Almost anything can become an instrument of evil in the wrong hands." Elijah gave them a compassionate look. "So, did you kids know Jessica Nolt?"

They all nodded.

"Well, can you tell me about her? Like what did she like to do for fun? Who were her closest friends? Stuff like that."

"She hung out with Daniel and Kasey and Geoffrey," one answered.

"They're over there by the horses," another said.

"They go to town sometimes," one of the girls added. "And to parties."

"Yes, they do," another boy confirmed. "They are on *Rumspringa*."

"Any idea what they do in town?" Elijah followed the kids' gaze to a group of three older teens sitting on a fence rail. Geoffrey, Daniel and Kasey, he presumed.

"We don't know. They don't really talk to us."

"Are they good kids? Do they go to singings and do their chores?"

The kids exchanged quick glances, probably afraid to answer and get their older friends in a pickle.

"Come on," he encouraged them. "I'm not here to get anyone in trouble. I'm just trying to see if I can figure out where Jessica was the day before she died."

"*Jah,* they are good. But you should ask them your questions." A boy pointed to the kids on the fence rail.

"Okay." He smiled and backed away. But the young kids scattered as if the porch had caught fire.

What was that all about? I'm not that scary.

But when he turned to go talk to the other group of kids, he understood why they had run off. Just down the hill, the bishop was coming toward him. So the meeting hadn't kept him away after all. And now his *Dat* had come to send him home. Some things would never change. Once the bishop decided on something, he never changed his mind.

Accepting his own son's decisions wouldn't be any different.

Elijah's heart sank. If he left the gathering, how could he protect Hannah? Didn't anyone understand that she was in danger and that they needed help and protection from something beyond their borders? But even his fear of leaving Hannah unprotected couldn't compete with his fear of the conversation about to take place.

His heart pounded in his chest like a drum and his throat grew so tight he could barely take in the air he needed. After eleven years, his *Dat* was coming to speak to him. He'd dreamed of this moment. Imagined it over and over in his mind in many different ways…none of the scenarios had ever ended well. He doubted this would, either.

He stood frozen to his spot on John's porch and waited. There was no smile on his *Dat*'s face, no welcome in his manners. Not that Eli had expected otherwise, but he had hoped somehow for a miracle. He still believed in them. As his father grew nearer, his appearance shocked Elijah. How old he'd grown. The lines on his face deeper, his hair whiter, his shoulders rounder. He stopped a few steps away, squared his feet under himself and crossed his arms over his chest.

"I know why you have come and about the recommendation of Chief McClendon, who is a good friend to our People. I spoke to the elders. We give you three days. After that, you will leave." His words were sharp and spoken in the Pennsylvania Dutch. And as soon as they were said, he dropped his arms, turned and started to march away.

Elijah shook his head at the unfeeling encounter. *Three days.* He wished they were already past.

Hi, Dat. *Good to see you,* Dat. *Miss you, too,* Dat.

Yeah, right.

Almost as if he'd heard the words, the bishop stopped and turned. Eli's heart jumped for a second as his father opened his mouth to speak again. *"Und kleine Pistole,"* the bishop added, marching away. "It isn't our way."

Eli swallowed away the hurt of his father's cold words and manner. Then he glanced over at his sister's buggy where he'd stowed away his Glock.

Of course, Dat, *no guns. If someone shoots at us again, I'll just hit him with a farm tool.* He broke no law by having a gun. He had not taken vows. And if that cop so many years ago had not shot his abductor, he and his sister, Abigail, would both be dead. Did that not mean anything to his father? Did the bishop not see that protecting the innocent was a good thing?

Elijah dropped his head and walked toward the other small group of teens.

"Elijah Miller, after all these years?" Margaret Brenneman whispered to Hannah as they cleared away the evening meal dishes. "I heard he showed up completely unannounced. That must have given you quite a shock."

"Yes, a little," Hannah answered.

"Wonder why he's back after all this time," Margaret continued, not really listening to Hannah's answer.

"And wasn't he always a favorite of yours?" Mary Payne jumped into the conversation. "In fact, if I remember correctly we were all astonished when you announced your engagement to Peter Nolt instead of to him."

"I'm sure I can't remember anything that happened so long ago," Hannah said, a little angry at their choice of topics. "It is surely of no consequence now. Peter is gone. Jessica is gone."

Hannah walked quickly to the kitchen with her stack of plates, hoping Margaret and Mary would give up their gossiping mission by the time she returned, but it seemed that was not to be.

"Levi says Elijah is staying with you during his visit?" Mary Payne added.

Hannah cringed. She hated any sort of gossip, but she especially hated it when the gossip involved her. And she could see exactly where this topic was leading. She wanted to silence their tongues. "He is estranged from his father. You know that. And he's here on business. Perhaps you should ask him about it yourself. 'Tis no secret."

"About that troubled Jessica, no doubt," Margaret said. "I've heard all sorts of tales of her goings-on at parties and such. It must make it all so difficult for you."

"Not a bit of truth in any of that talk. Idle prattle, I assure you." Hannah sighed in frustration at the turn in the conversation. "Jessica was a good girl."

"Of course she was, dear." Margaret shot Mary a worried look. "It must be such a terrible time for you."

"It's been difficult," Hannah said, lifting her chin high. "It was so unexpected."

Mary came and patted her hand. "And it can't help with all of this terrible talk going around. Well, at least you can count on the two of us not to join in."

Mary and Margaret saw the sadness in her eyes and finally turned to their work. Hannah wanted to flee, but forced herself to stay and help them with the dishes.

"Do you think you'll stay on at the Nolts' now that she's gone?" Mary started again.

"Where else would I go?" Hannah felt her tears begin to form. Normally, she wouldn't listen to such silly talk, but today, after all she'd been through, she didn't need to hear this from these women, who had nothing better to do than speculate about her business.

"You have kinfolk in the town of Esperance, do you not?" Mary said.

"A cousin." What was this? Hannah shuddered at their words. They wanted her sent away. Out of their sight.

She could take no more. She rushed from the kitchen before the tears came. Abigail was just coming into the house. She nearly knocked her over.

"I'm sorry. I'm so sorry."

"Hannah, what is it?" It only took Abigail a second to look past her into the kitchen and see Mary and Margaret there. "What did they say to you, those gossiping twits?"

Hannah tried to stop her tears. How foolish she felt to be rattled by the silliest women in all of Willow Trace. "There was talk about Jessica. Bad talk. They were suggesting I go to Esperance to live with my cousin."

"I ought to give them a piece of my mind," Abigail said. "You're not going anywhere. Come, Hannah. Let us walk and take in some fresh air. It's gotten much too crowded in here." She said the last part loudly so that the other ladies could hear.

Hannah took Abigail's arm and they walked out behind the farmhouse.

At least, they were giving him three days, Elijah thought. That was more time than he'd expected. He almost laughed thinking how upset Thomas Nolt would be having to put up with him for a few more days. Eli gazed over the others at the gathering. He wondered if anyone had seen the awkward encounter with his father.

No. The men were chatting and putting the tables away, the women cleaning.

He continued to look around, checking for Hannah regularly. He did not see her. Nor Abigail. Nor Thomas, for that matter. In fact, Elijah hadn't seen Thomas since the meal had begun, and that surprised him since the entire day his old friend had been quite intent to make certain that he and Hannah did not get within a stone's throw of each other. Thomas was hiding something, of that Eli was certain. He feared it might have to do with the horrible things happening to Hannah. He could indeed picture Thomas as the man atop the fleeing steed he'd spotted racing off from the cottage. But what he couldn't imagine was Thomas knocking Hannah to the floor and hurting her. In fact, he couldn't imagine Thomas causing Hannah any harm whatsoever. Thomas cared for Hannah greatly. That was not debatable. Still, where was Thomas? Why wasn't he keeping a better eye on Hannah? Or perhaps they were together now? Eli had to admit he didn't like that idea one bit, and it made him all the more anxious to find them.

But first he needed to talk to the other friends of Jessica's. With only three days, he had no time to spare. So far, the only thing he had to go on was a big pony sale and a journal that, from the stairwell, he had overheard Hannah telling Thomas she knew nothing about. Two things, which added up to nothing.

Elijah moved toward the other group of teens— Daniel, Kasey and Geoffrey. Daniel Hostetler was easy to pick of the three. The Hostetler family had been around forever, every one of them tall, lanky and dark-headed. And interesting that no one other than Thomas had bothered to mention that Jessica had had a boyfriend. He wondered what else they hadn't told him.

Eli approached them quickly.

"Hello, Daniel. I'm Elijah Miller. I went to school with your sister Miriam. I heard she married and moved away to Indiana." Eli reached out his hand and gave the kid a firm shake.

"That's the truth." The teen avoided looking him in the eye but returned the handshake with gusto.

"I'm Geoffrey Payne." The other boy stood from the fence and offered a hand to Elijah. "My family moved here from Ohio a few years back. We live on the other side of your cousin John. John told us that you're a cop—Internal Affairs, ain't so?"

Eli nodded.

Geoffrey smiled. "And this is Kasey Phelps. She's staying with the Lapp family for the year."

"Hi." Elijah shook her hand. "I understand you all were close friends to Jessica Nolt?"

Kasey and Geoffrey nodded with long, sad faces.

"I'm hear to look into—"

"*Jah,* we heard why you are here from John Miller," Geoffrey interrupted. "But we don't know anything."

"That's for sure. We don't know anything," Daniel said. "I used to see Jessica a lot. We courted, you know. But she broke it off with me. Didn't see her much after that."

So, were they courting or weren't they? Elijah listened to the strained inflections in Daniel's voice.

"Did you see her last week?" he asked the group.

"No." They all shook their heads, but looked away. Elijah had a suspicion that one or more of them were not telling the truth now. Maybe all of them.

"Did you know if she kept a journal?" He continued with his short list of questions.

"A journal?" Daniel repeated, forcing out a nervous laugh. "Like something you jot down thoughts in?"

"Yeah, a journal."

"I don't know anything about a journal. Do you?" Daniel looked at his friends.

They shook their heads. "No."

"So, when did you last see—?"

"Oh. Gash. Sorry. I hear my *Dat* calling," Daniel interrupted. "Have to go help. I'll find you guys later." The tall boy ran off, down the green, grassy hill and toward the long line of buggies getting ready to depart before dark.

"He still gets really upset talking about Jessica," Kasey said.

"I understand." Eli nodded. "But maybe you can tell me more about her?"

Kasey nodded. "She was so nice, a really good girl. Always trying to help people. I still can't believe she's gone. I keep thinking she'll be sitting there with us, coming to the next singing, you know?"

"Did the four of you hang out often?"

"Sure. Almost every Saturday," Geoffrey said.

"What did you guys do?"

"You know, the usual courtin' stuff. Dinner in Strasbourg. Sometimes we'd see a movie. A couple of parties. But none of us really like that sort of thing so much."

"Did you go with Jessica into the city the night before she died?"

"No. That was a Monday night. I work at the SuperMart on Mondays until eight," Geoffrey said. "Every Monday."

"Me, too," Kasey added. "Anyway, Jessica had her accident in the barn, didn't you know? She didn't go out."

Elijah chose to change the subject. "What's in the city?" he asked them. "Why might Jessica have wanted to go there?"

"Well, a few weeks ago, Jess started spending time with an *Englischer* friend she met at a *Rumspringa* party." Geoffrey shrugged. "Supposedly the girl was from Philadelphia."

"Does this *Englischer* friend have a name?"

"Brittney," Kasey said.

"Brittney Baker," Geoffrey said.

"You remember her last name?" Kasey looked at Geoffrey with a wounded expression. "You never remember anything."

Geoffrey shrugged. "Sometimes I remember stuff."

Kasey jumped off the fence rail and pouted. "Yeah, he remembers because she's drop-dead gorgeous. Very exotic looking—long dark hair, long legs, big eyes."

Eli tried not to smile at the lovers' spat. "And she's from Philly?"

"That's what Jess said. We never really talked to her. Only saw her *once* at that *one* party." Geoffrey emphasized the important words to Kasey.

"But you think Jessica saw her again?" he asked.

"She told us that she did." Kasey narrowed her eyes. "Hey, why so many questions about Jessica's friend? She died in the stable, right?"

"Her clothing and other evidence suggest that may not have been the complete truth," Elijah said carefully.

The two kids looked at each other, but didn't say anything else.

Eli frowned. "Sorry for all the questions. The police are just trying to do a little more research since it's not clear exactly what happened. Um… but you must have talked this through with the local police and your deacons, right?"

"No," Kasey said with a thoughtful air. "You're the first person to ask us anything."

Geoffrey nodded in accordance.

Eli thought back to the illegible notes in Jessica's investigative file. Maybe they were illegible because the conversations never actually took place. "Was Jessica close with any other Amish in this area? Any other teens?"

"She was friends with everyone. But she and Daniel were steady, you know," Kasey said. "She spent all her free time with him—well, until she broke it off."

"So she did break it off?"

"*Jah.* He was crushed. Thought she'd found another beau."

Like mother, like daughter. "And when did that happen?"

"Just a few weeks ago."

It sounded to Elijah as if Jessica had met her friend Brittney about the same time as when she broke things off with Daniel. He pressed his lips together, wondering how hard it would be to find this Brittney Baker of Philadelphia. It would be important to speak with her. "One last question. Did Jessica keep a journal that you know of?"

The kids shook their head with vehemence. "In this *Ordnung,* you aren't allowed to keep journals. Too much inward reflection."

"Right. But it doesn't mean that no one has one."

"It means that Jessica didn't have one," Kasey said back.

"Okay. Thank you." Elijah pulled out his phone and sent a quick text to Tucci, asking him to dig up any information he could find on a Brittney Baker living in Philadelphia. When he finished, he saw other men in the distance clearing away the tables and benches. It was time to go. And he should lend a hand with the work and thank his cousin John. "Well, if you think of anything else, I'll be at the Nolts' for another night or two."

He turned away and headed toward the buggies. He still had not spotted Hannah or Thomas, and this was starting to make him nervous. Everyone should be gathered below ready to head home. Where were they? He spotted Abigail by her horse and buggy. She was talking to a young man, but it was not Thomas. Eli scanned the farm. It was growing dark. The sun had begun to set and cast an orange-red glow over the land around him.

There. At the top of the hill behind the farmhouse, he spotted a man large enough to be Thomas. He needed to tell him about his father's decree and the three days. Moving quickly, he rounded the house and started upward. But as he climbed higher he saw that the man was not Amish. Or at least not dressed Plain but only wearing a black Amish dress hat like the one Nicolas had found in the woods the day before. He was tall, and gripped a small rod or a stick of some sort in his left hand.

A spurt of adrenaline shot through Elijah. Was this their shooter come to seek Hannah out again? Or did he already have Hannah? Elijah tore up the big hill. No way would this guy get away from him this time.

NINE

Elijah knew the land, and on the other side of that hill was nothing but open fields in every direction. There was nowhere for this man to go. No road to hide a car on. He would have him.

Elijah was close enough now to see that the man was tall, but fair and much too thin to have been Thomas. He spotted Elijah coming at him. He turned immediately and headed over the back of the hill. It didn't matter. There was nowhere for him to go. Elijah was nearly there.

He topped the hill and looked down over the vast pastures on the other side. He saw cows and sheep and goats and acres and acres of grassy fields. There was no man.

Impossible. Impossible. It was as if he'd chased a ghost. Only he didn't believe in ghosts. He'd seen someone and just like yesterday that person had vanished.

Defeated, Elijah dropped his gaze to the ground. Beside him in the grass he saw the stick.

It was the right size to have been the one the man had carried. He must have tossed it aside in his flight.

Elijah picked it up. It was nothing special, just an ordinary stick one would find on the forest floor. Fresh dirt clung to the small end. Elijah's focus switched back to the earth. Perhaps the tall man had been digging. To his right, he found not a hole but several deliberate markings drawn into the rich soil. Elijah stepped back and studied the image. It was a symbol he knew well—a Dutch hex sign. Hex signs came in many forms but his one was in the shape of an eight-pointed star. It was encompassed in a large circle except for the north point, which extended beyond the circle's arch.

He studied the symbol for a moment, wondering what kind of message could be meant from it. The meaning of Dutch hex symbols had long been a source of confusion, even in Lancaster where these painted designs often hung on houses and barns. Many believed them to be nothing more than a decorative pattern. In fact, some of the patterns were sewn into quilts or painted on wood and sold to tourists. But other folks thought there was some religious attachment to the symbol. But what that religious significance was no one seemed to agree over. Still, this uninvited man who'd been watching over them had taken the time to draw it into the ground and in a manner of speaking had lured him up there to look at it. Perhaps it was some sort of clue? A warning?

Elijah pulled out his cell phone and snapped a picture of the design. He messaged it to Tucci with a message.

In addition to Brittney Baker. Check this out. Another uninvited visitor. Male. Thin. Over six feet. Fair skin. Ran off, but left this symbol where he was standing. Please reference. Will call later.

A few seconds later, Tucci wrote back that he would.

Leaving the hilltop, Elijah turned back to the crowd on the other side of the farmhouse. And at long last he saw Hannah and Thomas standing with Abigail. Well, at least Hannah was safe. But this case was getting more complicated by the minute, and Eli was beginning to think that three days would never be enough to figure out the mysteries of Willow Trace.

Hannah stood away from the others, pretending to busy herself folding and refolding a quilt that she and some of the other women had spent the afternoon working on, all the while staying close enough to listen while Elijah and Thomas talked.

"I have a meet with the elders this evening,"

Thomas said to Elijah. "Mother wants to tag along and chat with the other women. If you and your sister would be good enough to take Hannah back to Nolt Cottage, we'd welcome both of you as our guests tonight."

"We'd be delighted to take Hannah home," Abigail answered quickly.

"Denki," Hannah said to Abigail. She did not look at Elijah for fear Thomas would see those feelings in her, which she did not want exposed.

"I will join you soon." Thomas turned and left them.

Abigail smiled and sang a sweet tune as she checked the hitch and reins, readying the buggy for the drive home. Hannah hoped they would allow her to sit in the back. She couldn't imagine a twenty-minute ride giving Elijah Miller the view of her bare neck. She was uncomfortable merely thinking of it. Even now as he took the quilt from her hands to place it in the carriage, she felt herself trembling with nerves.

"Here you go, brother." Abigail handed him the reins. "I hope you remember how to drive."

"Huh? Where are *you* going?" His face showed genuine confusion.

"Mr. Phelps's cousin from Indiana is visiting for the spring. He's a widower," she explained. "He's asked me to Strasbourg this evening for an ice cream."

"You're going on a date?" Elijah's eyes widened.

"We call it courtin'." She smiled at Hannah. "Make sure he doesn't traumatize my mare, would ya? I'll see you all first thing in the morning. Thank Thomas for his kind offer, but my house is much closer to Strasbourg than yours. I like Mr. Phelps, but I don't know if I like him enough to drive me all the way back to Nolt Cottage. Anyway, once he sees that Hannah is five times sweeter and prettier than I am, he'll be inviting her for an ice cream. So I might as well enjoy the attention while I can."

"Not so." Hannah blushed. How could Abigail say such a thing?

Abigail gave her brother a hug and headed down the long line of buggies toward the Phelps family.

Elijah turned to her and offered her a hand up into the buggy. His light touch over her fingers sent a tingle across her arm.

"You enjoyed the gathering?" she said.

"I did." He moved in beside her and tapped the reins to Abigail's mare, urging the horse forward.

They rode in silence, one by one separating from the other family buggies. Evening was upon them. The sun had sunk low and filled the sky with a purple glow. Every so often he glanced at her, his eyes bright and his smile dazzling in the evening shadows.

"So, it was *gut* to see your family?" she repeated, feeling that such a long silence had become awkward.

"Yes. It was fine." His head dropped a little. "Although my *Dat* came to the gathering, ya know?"

"I did not know," she said with a smile. "I did not see him there. But he came to greet you. How nice—"

"He didn't come to greet me, Hannah," Elijah interrupted. "He came to say that I have three days to find out whatever I need to know and then I have to leave whether I'm finished or not. So now might be a good time for you to tell me all about that journal and everything else."

"Yes. I would have done so this morning but Nana came in. Then you and Mr. McClendon went to the stable to..." A dry lump filled her throat. "So, how did you know about the journal?"

"I could hear you," he explained. "I could hear you and Thomas talking this morning over breakfast."

"Everything?" Heat crept up her neck as she remembered Thomas's jealousy and innuendos of her feelings toward Elijah.

"I heard what I needed to hear," he said.

What was that supposed to mean? She turned away, her face flushing with warmth. She was thankful Mary and Margaret the gossips weren't there to see her blushing.

"And a good thing, too," he continued, oblivious of her embarrassment. "With only three days to figure out what's going on around here, I can't afford to waste a second. Neither can you. Don't play games, Hannah. I need to know everything, so start talking. Don't leave out a thing."

"I do not play games, as you say."

He cut his eyes at her. He was not happy.

"I have wanted to tell you, Elijah. It's just that…" She pressed her lips together. "I didn't realize the danger."

"Obviously."

"You have to understand we thought we were doing the right thing in protecting our traditions and keeping all of this out of the press. Seems ignorant now. I apologize." She looked off into the evening, thinking sadly about her stepdaughter. "In any case, I don't know about a journal. When the man last night asked for one, it was the first time I had ever heard of such a thing. But that doesn't mean she did not have one. Maybe her friends would know about it. I saw you talking with them."

"They said they didn't know about a journal. I asked. But I don't know that they were telling the absolute truth."

Hannah looked down, shaking her head. She

should have known her own daughter better. "She was on *Rumspringa*. I gave her every freedom. I did not ask questions or give her cautions. I should have."

"Hannah, I know you want to blame yourself, but until you know what you're dealing with, I think that's premature and, frankly, it's a waste of the little time we have to get this straight." His eyes stayed focused on the road. "I think we should make a search for this journal. If she had one, it must be around somewhere. But hidden in a place where you and Thomas and Nana Ruth would never look."

"How about in the barn since I found her there? Maybe the person who hit me the morning I found Jessica was already looking for this journal when I arrived for milking."

"There was someone in the barn when you found the body? I don't remember reading that in the police report. Well, if you could call that a report. Did you know that Jessica's friends haven't even been questioned about Jessica before?"

"No. They wouldn't have been. McClendon knew we didn't want an investigation."

"Then what? He changed his mind and had the governor send me here?"

"I do not know about that." Hannah stopped a moment, realizing why maybe the horse sale to the governor might have seemed relevant. But what could Thomas possibly have to do with this? "And McClendon didn't even know about the person in the barn. So it would not have been in the police report. I didn't tell anyone but Thomas. And he—"

"Told you not to tell anyone?"

"Jah." Hannah dropped her head. "Like I said. We did not know the danger."

"Someone attacked you in the barn and you didn't think there was a danger?"

"I'm sorry, Elijah. I don't understand any of this, either. That much I can promise you."

"I know."

"What about the journal?"

"I don't know if the journal would actually be in the barn. Whoever is after it most likely already looked there, and we know they haven't found it."

Hannah looked down. "Can I ask you something which I do not understand?"

"Sure."

"Why do you think they brought her to us and left her in the barn? Thomas said that she could not have died in the barn because there was not enough blood. God forbid, if someone did kill her and they did it somewhere else, why bring her home?"

"A good question. And unfortunately there could be a million answers to that. For example, to look for this so-called journal. To scare you. Because the Amish don't pursue killers and that would give the event a low profile. Can you imagine the press if she'd been found outside the community?"

"I cannot." She knew very little of the world outside Willow Trace. How different she was from Elijah. How naive and simple he must find her.

"Whatever the reason, it is a threat that says, 'We can get to you.' As they keep proving over and over."

A threat. Hannah swallowed hard. "I—I hadn't thought about that," she said.

"And a black car? Like the one Nicholas saw? You saw one, didn't you?"

She nodded. "I'm sorry. I should have told you as soon as you arrived. It's just that I'd promised Thomas."

She went on to tell Elijah about Jessica's strange behavior before her death. He listened in a detached, businesslike manner, which felt cold to her after his tenderness to her the evening before. That should not make her sad, she told herself. But then again, since he'd arrived her thoughts were not always where they should be.

"Tell me more about Daniel Hostetler. Why did Jessica break it off with him?"

Hannah shook her head. "I do not have an

answer to that. She told me that she didn't want to spend her whole *Rumspringa* in the same courtship—that she needed to branch out. That always seemed less than the complete truth to me. But like I said, I didn't push her."

"Was it like Jessica to want to take a break? To want to have a lot of freedom?"

"No. It wasn't. She was very much like me in that way. Very loyal. No matter what people are saying about her now."

"You consider yourself loyal?" Elijah huffed.

"I don't want to quarrel about the past." *And I don't want to cry in front of you again.* But she felt the tears coming. His comment, though, almost made her angry. He could think what he wanted. He didn't know she thought not only for herself but for him, too. He didn't know she couldn't have children. That she could never give him the family he'd said he wanted. And he had wanted a family. He had told her that many times when they talked of their future together.

"I don't, either, Hannah. It's okay. You did hurt me, but that was a long time ago. I was torn between the two worlds and you made the decision easy. If you and I had married, well…it doesn't matter."

"It was not an easy decision." She blinked back the tears. "But you know how I made it?"

"I don't. I don't think we've talked much since," he teased.

"*Jah,* that is true."

"So, tell me…why Peter?"

"He needed me more than you did."

"Because of Jessica?"

She nodded. "I couldn't imagine leaving her. I didn't want to leave her. And Peter, God rest his soul, was a good man and a good father and a good husband."

Elijah turned to her. He reached for her hand and gave it a squeeze. "You made a good choice, Hannah. I never questioned that. I just missed you."

"I am sorry—" Hannah shook her head.

"It was the right choice, Hannah. We don't need to talk of it again," he said. "I'll be gone soon and all will be as it was. You'll marry Thomas soon. He loves you. And I'll go back to doing the work that God called me to do."

You are wrong. You have come back into my life now. Nothing will be as it was. She kept her thoughts inside and turned her head so that he might not read them from her expression. "And you? Any hope for a family? I was most surprised yesterday when you said that you did not have any children."

Eli laughed. "I did used to talk of that, didn't I? No. Never happened. I probably work too hard and what woman could put up with me for a lifetime? And children are such a handful—I'd probably make a mess of being a parent."

She smiled. "Jessica was wonderful. But I suppose there was much I did not know about her. I saw you talking to her friends. I wanted so badly to ask them questions myself. But I know that would only create more talk."

"Did you know Jessica had a friend named Brittney in the city?"

Hannah turned to him wide-eyed. "No. In the city? I didn't even know she had been to the city."

She tried not to feel hurt by discovering that Jessica had kept secrets from her. It was normal for a girl at that age to break away from her parents. But it all seemed so shocking and unexpected. At least, it took her mind from thoughts of Elijah. Well, sort of.

"Would it make you feel better to travel with me into Philadelphia tomorrow? My partner, Mitchell Tucci, is finding out where this young lady lives—this friend of Jessica's. I'm going to find her and see what she knows. I think you should come with me."

"Me? In the city?" Hannah almost laughed.

"Yes. You in the city."

"I don't know. I doubt Thomas will agree."

"Well, then I'll just have to insist— Whooooooah, girl!" Elijah grasped at the reins as Abigail's mare spooked and pulled the vehicle so hard to the left that Hannah slammed up against his side. Her stomach leapt into her throat.

"We need to turn here." She pointed to the gravel path to the Nolts' cottage. "If you can manage it."

"The mare does seem mighty reluctant, doesn't she?" Elijah held fast to the reins and steadied the horse. She slowed her steps and proceeded but with much hesitation. Elijah tapped her rear with his crop and urged her on again with a strong voice. "You know my car never fights me like this."

"Maybe you're just out of practice." Hannah reached over. "Hand me the reins I'll take it from here."

"Are you kidding me? I used to race these buggies." He kept the reins from her. "I haven't forgotten a thing."

"I remember." She eyed him. "I remember you used to lose races."

They both laughed. He looked down on her with a kind smile. The first one he'd shown her since the ride home started. A spark of heat flushed through her core.

Three days, she reminded herself. In three days Elijah Miller would be back in the city where he belonged. He wasn't one of them. She knew that fact as well as he did. They had made their choices years ago and could never be together now. No matter what her heart seemed to be thinking.

Hannah's laughter sounded sweet to his ears. He would gladly have listened to it all evening. Every evening. Any evening, for that matter.

Time with family, good hard work, fine people with no agenda other than to help one another, Hannah's smile and laughter—those were things that would have been a part of his life every day if she'd agreed to marry him, if he hadn't left the *Ordnung*. Boy! Today had been a big fat dose of all the things he missed. Part of him wanted to share all that was in his heart with Hannah and tell her how the experience had moved him— how she moved him. How he loved the chance just to sit next to her in the buggy. Alone. Listening to her laugh and catching flashes of her beautiful smile.

But the other part of him was wary and bitter. And angry at his own heart for being so tender toward her. He couldn't take any more tears and confessions. She had crushed his feelings, refused him, yet made it impossible for him to love another woman. And now with one explanation, with one breath he was forgiving her everything? Inviting her to the city with him? Sitting beside her and thinking of nothing but how sweet her laughter was? Maybe three days was too long for his weakening heart. Maybe he was in more danger than Hannah—in danger of falling in love and getting hurt again.

Just get her back to the cottage, Miller, he told himself. If only this silly mare of Abigail's could keep a steady pace, he would. But as it was, he could barely keep her moving straight ahead. Hannah seemed amused by the animal's behavior, but more and more Elijah was beginning to suspect there was something to the horse's skittishness.

"I should have insisted we take my car," he muttered under his breath, grabbing the blanket from the back of the buggy—the blanket that concealed his Glock 19. He thought of the man on the hill who'd disappeared. A lookout to see when they were coming? To be sure they hadn't been at home? There was something to it. "I have a bad feeling about this."

"Maybe the mare is not used to being driven at night?" Hannah suggested.

"No. Something's not right." His body tensed. "She sees or smells something we don't."

"Like an animal?"

"Yes." *A two-legged one,* he wanted to say, but didn't want to scare her in case he was merely being paranoid. If they could just get past this front part of the farm where the woods were thick and enclosed them, he'd feel much better. But there was another five hundred yards or so to go and—

Eli caught a flash of movement in his peripheral, something shiny in the forest reflecting the buggy's headlights. He stiffened. He wasn't being paranoid. Someone was there. Animals didn't run around in the woods with shiny metal.

"Sit back, Hannah." He cracked his whip over the mare again, asking her to move forward. The faster they got through that canopy of trees, the better. The mare bolted forward as if she sensed danger, too.

Even Hannah seemed on alert. She grabbed on to his arm. "You're right! There's a car coming at us!"

Eli spotted the car but it was too late. Its lights flashed bright as it tore out of the woods and turned directly toward their buggy. Elijah could see nothing but white. His ears heard nothing but Hannah's scream.

The mare whinnied, jerked forward, then kicked back. The front of the buggy lifted from the ground, then titled to the right as the horse balked again and pulled them toward the grassy ditch. The car continued straight for them. Elijah reached for Hannah. It looked like they would have to jump. He pulled her against him, but hesitated as the car swerved hard to the left at the last second, just missing the horse.

The car did not, however, miss hitting the buggy. Its back fender caught the front left wheel and the wooden spokes crunched and split like twigs.

"Take the reins," he shouted to Hannah.

Elijah aimed his Glock at the back of the vehicle. Time to find out who that was and put an end to all of these unwanted visits to Lancaster. How dare anyone come into this safe haven and cause such havoc and fear to the people he loved? Anger pulsed hot through his veins as he shot at the car's back tire. The driver shot back, hitting the taillight on the buggy. It shattered to bits, exploding like the anger inside him. He fired again. This time he succeeded in blowing out the back left wheel, which caused the car to spin. The driver could no longer shoot but was forced to focus on steering. Elijah knew if could also hit the front tire he could possibly stall the car and driver long enough to approach them. Elijah raised his gun to the front end of the car, but the swaying buggy wouldn't give him a clean shot.

Hannah had not been able to take control of the reins. Unguided, the mare recoiled at the gunfire and tugged the collapsing buggy farther into the ditch. Elijah swept his hand down to grab the loose reins, but there was nothing to be done—the buggy was toppling over.

"Jump!" He took hold of Hannah's arm and pulled her from the moving vehicle.

TEN

Elijah took hold of Hannah's arm with a strong grip and lifted her from the floor of the buggy. As the vehicle began to roll on its side, he pushed her through the driver's-side door, then followed with a great leap of his own. They hit the gravel path as the buggy tumbled and slid into the deep ditch.

"You okay?"

Hannah didn't answer. Ignoring the gravel that seemed to have embedded itself in her palms and face as it had his own, she hopped up and raced toward the front of the buggy.

"What are you doing?" he called after her. "You're going to get hurt." She was much too close to the anxious mare, which seemed to be pinned under the hitch. "Let her calm down."

"She can't calm down. She has to be set free. Otherwise she'll hurt or kill herself, if she hasn't already." Hannah moved on, ignoring him as she reached for something behind the crazed beast.

Elijah cringed but moved in behind her, ready to yank her from harm's way if need be.

"Hannah, come on away from there. Let her be."

But determined to help the stressed horse, she continued to bend over the joint, working her arm at the hitch and harness.

Stubborn woman.

Finally a *click* sounded and Abigail's mare took off down the road at a full gallop, still in her harness with the reins flapping behind her. Within seconds she was out of sight.

"She could still hurt herself." Hannah turned as he sidled up next to her. "But chances are she'll find her way home or to another barn and we'll get her back."

Elijah didn't care about the mare. He didn't care about the trashed buggy or Thomas or Abigail or his *Dat.* He didn't care about anything that had been on his mind of late. He put his hands on her arms and pulled her closer. "We could have been crushed. That was no grazing bullet. That was meant to end us. What do these people want, Hannah? Tell me now so that I can help you." *I don't want to lose you again.*

"I don't know. I don't know." She trembled against him. "I told you everything."

He pressed her closer—close enough to feel her breath on his shoulder. Close enough to take in her scent and feel her warmth. Together they stood in each other's arms, trembling.

Hannah tried to wiggle from his tight embrace, but he knew she needed to feel him as much as he needed her. She was as frightened as that mare. As he stroked her shoulder, she relaxed and leaned against him, her wet, warm tears soaking the collar of his shirt.

"I've lost everything," she whispered. "Everything."

Her words and the feel of her against him slowed his racing adrenaline. "I felt like that a bit today, Hannah. Looking around at all I gave up when I left here. You have lost a lot. But you haven't lost everything. You still have your love and compassion and your drive to help others. You have a lot, Hannah Kurtz."

She laughed as he used her maiden name. "No one has called me that in a long, long time."

"Yeah, well, you'll always be Hannah Kurtz to me. No matter who you marry."

He tightened his arms around her. He kissed the top of her head. How he had loved this woman—and how he loved her still. It made him ache to see her suffering so deeply. Anger and fear coursed through him, too. This was his home, his people and his heritage. This was Hannah, *his* Hannah. He would keep her safe—even though he'd never see her again after these three days.

"Lord, give Hannah the strength to endure this hard time in her life. Keep her safe and protect her from these people who wish her harm. Lead us to this journal so we can move forward and restore the joy in living for You."

Hannah nodded her head against his chest, as he prayed, her tears still streaming. "Thank you, Elijah Miller. Thank you for being here with me at this time. I know that the Lord has brought you to me."

"I wouldn't be anywhere else," he whispered. "Now let's get you home." He took a flashlight from the broken buggy and turned them down the path, the flashlight in one hand, Hannah's hand in his other.

With each step toward Nolt Cottage, Hannah's fear and panic slipped away. Elijah's hand seemed to feed her his strength and courage as they walked together. The other more tender sentiments released from his touch she tried to dismiss.

"I'm glad Thomas and Nana Ruth will be coming to the cottage from the other direction. I wouldn't want them to see the wreckage."

Eli nodded, looking back at the destroyed buggy. "I know. And I dread telling Abby."

"Abigail will understand. And if I know Thomas, he will take care of everything for her.

That's how he is." She stopped and pressed her lips together. "Your prayer was most kind. I didn't know you were still in the faith."

"Living in the world doesn't mean I have to be of the world," he said. "It's harder. There's more distractions to be sure, but I think in the end not joining the church has made my faith strong, not weakened it."

Hannah almost smiled. "But that doesn't fit too well with Amish thinking, does it?"

"No. I don't suppose it does. I guess you could say I have a tolerance for other life choices. I think there are good English people who love God as much as we do. For me, being Amish isn't a choice to have faith or not to have faith," he said. "It's a choice of how and maybe even where we are called to live."

"But how do you give reason for the gun and the taking of human life? This is a part of your job, no?"

"No. Well, the gun, yes. But the gun is for protection. I've never killed anyone. Don't want to, either."

"Would you? Would you kill someone? You fired the gun tonight, did you not?"

"I shot at the tires of the car. I was trying to stop them. Not kill them. But I'm not so sure they weren't trying to kill us this time."

"They weren't before?"

"I don't think so. Tonight was different. The attack, it was much more aggressive. More risky. More dangerous. They have upped the ante and I don't know why. Maybe we are on to them and we don't even know it." He laughed.

"On to them? Upped the ante? Sometimes it's hard to remember you were here among us once."

"Sometimes I feel that way. But not today, Hannah. Not today. The gathering was nice. Thank you for insisting that I go. I'm glad I did."

"I knew you would be…and seeing your *Dat?* Not as bad as you anticipated, no?"

"The verdict is still out on that."

"There you go again, with your strange expressions."

Elijah stopped on the gravel path and turned his head toward the horse stable. "Is that…?"

She followed his dark gaze to the holding pen. Abigail's chestnut mare paced back and forth in front of the gate. "I told you she wouldn't go far. Let's go and bring her in."

They made their way behind the horse, guided her to the holding pen, then removed her harness. She snorted and paced between them still very agitated, but at least they had found her.

"I'll go fetch a lantern from the kitchen. Then we can take her to a stall and give her some hay.

She will feel better to be with the other horses inside, *jah?*" Hannah gave him a slight smile, glad to have a task to fix her mind on. She turned away toward the house.

Elijah grabbed her by the elbow. "You're braver than you should be. I'll go with you."

She did not like the wariness in his eyes. They'd already been attacked and shot at. What else could happen in one evening? It must have been tiresome to go through life worried about one's safety at every turn. Hannah had always been thankful for the safe haven that was her Amish community, but now even more so. If this was what life was like on the outside, she wanted no part of it. Elijah's presence might produce sparks in her heart, but she would forgo that for a quiet place to serve the Lord. Right? Yes. She was sure of it. Perhaps she'd always been sure of it and that's why she'd chosen Jessica and Peter. Oh, why did she keep going back to that moment so long ago? Clearly, Elijah had let it go. Why couldn't she?

Eli walked quickly to the dark cottage. She could barely keep pace with his long strides. And despite her momentary flash of confidence, angst crept into her skin and filled her senses. Eli seemed tense, as well.

"What is it?" she asked.

"I thought I heard something." He reached back and took her hand.

"Fear thou not; for I am with thee," she began her favorite verse. *"Be not—"*

"Be not dismayed; for I am thy God," Eli interrupted. *"I will strengthen thee; yea, I will help thee; yea, I will uphold thee with the right hand of my righteousness."*

Hannah swallowed hard, looking up into his beautiful blue eyes. Remorse for the pain she'd caused him all those years ago sank her heart low and she closed her eyes against her regret.

"Don't fall apart on me now." He moved closer, offering his embrace but not forcing it upon her.

Hannah stepped back. "I'm—I'm sorry. I am just glad you are come. So glad you are here."

"Me, too." Eli tilted his head and lifted his arms again.

This time, Hannah sank into his embrace. She placed her hands on his chest and felt the steady beat of his heart. His arms surrounded her. And she felt...she felt safe.

After a long moment, he lifted her hand to his lips and kissed her fingers gently. "You need to rest, Hannah. You must be—"

Crash! They turned toward the back door. Something inside the house had fallen. Something big and heavy.

"Can't seem to get a break, can we?" Elijah

slipped his gun from its holster and slid open the back kitchen door.

"I didn't know you had brought the gun," she whispered.

"Would you feel better if I had left it in the buggy?" He stared back at her.

She shook her head no. She had to admit that although the gun made her uneasy, she would have felt worse without it. Once inside the kitchen, she clicked on the overhead oil-powered lights.

As soft light spilled over the room, they each sucked in a quick breath. Elijah was right to have followed her to the house. Someone had most definitely been inside and probably still was.

ELEVEN

"I think they're gone," Elijah whispered, putting an arm around Hannah as the tears spilled over her cheeks.

The house was a horrible chaos. Not one thing seemed to be in place. Tables and chairs had been overturned. The cupboard emptied. Flour and oats and other grains tossed and spread across the hardwood floors. The upholstered sofa had been shredded with a knife and unstuffed. Broken plates and kitchen utensils were strewn about. But the crash had come from the corner where Daniel Hostetler sat bound, gagged and duct-taped to one of the kitchen chairs. It looked as if in trying to free himself he'd turned his chair over and landed on his side.

Eli rushed to the young man and carefully lifted the tape from his mouth. "You okay?"

He nodded.

"Who did this? Are they still here?"

"I don't know. I don't think so."

Elijah frowned as he began to cut the boy loose. "So, what happened? How did you get here like this?"

Elijah righted the chair and helped Daniel up and into it, as there was nowhere else to sit. When Daniel did not answer, Elijah righted a few of the other chairs and pulled one next to the kid.

"Listen, Daniel, I let you run off earlier today, but I shouldn't have. Whatever you know about all this, you need to come clean. Now."

The kid swallowed hard. He lifted his eyes to Hannah, then back to Elijah. "But I—I don't really know anything."

Elijah folded his arms over his chest. "Then how did you end up here and in this chair?"

He looked at Hannah. There was shame in his eyes. Slowly, he reached into his shirt and pulled out a cloth bag with a drawstring top. "I—I was returning this."

Elijah took the bag and opened it. Inside was a large amount of cash in hundreds.

"Thomas's money!" Hannah ran over to the boy, covering her mouth with one hand. "Oh, Daniel, it was *you* in the house last night. I knew I had heard the voice before." She paused and looked confused. "But why? Why did you come in the night? Why not just come and ask for what you need? Why sneak in and scare me to death and hurt me? Thomas is always generous with his earnings. You must know that."

Daniel's head dropped below his shoulders, but still he said nothing.

"That's it." Elijah stood, grabbed his phone from his pocket and showed it to the kid. "Time to call Chief McClendon."

"No. Please. No." Daniel's voice sounded panicked. "They'll kill Mrs. Nolt. They'll kill me. I promised them I wouldn't talk to the police. They're watching me. I saw them at the gathering."

"The man on the hill?"

Daniel nodded. "Please don't call the police."

"So, who are these people? Why would they want to kill you or Hannah or Jessica? What is this journal that you keep talking about?"

"I don't know." He shrugged. "But Jessica took it and she shouldn't have. We have to find it. *I* have to find it."

"Did they say what's in this journal?" What could a young Amish girl take from *Englischers* that would have them willing to kill?

Daniel shook his head. "I don't know. I don't know," he said, nearly crying now. "They just keep telling me to get it."

Eli sighed heavily. He sat back in the chair across from Daniel, then motioned for Hannah to sit also. "Why don't you start at the beginning,

Daniel? Don't leave out a thing. When and how did these people come into your lives?"

Daniel nodded. "Well, you know that Jessica told me to not come a-callin' on her anymore. At first, I thought this was just her way. You know, to take some time and think us over a bit before we could...well, before we get real serious. But then I find out that she's going into town every chance she gets. I could not think why she would do this but that she had found herself another beau. So I—I followed her to town on the train one night."

"When was this, Daniel? What night?" Elijah asked.

"Two weeks ago."

Hannah covered her mouth again, this time to muffle a sob.

"Okay. Keep going," Elijah prompted him.

"So, she took the train. I followed her. She carried a large bag and walked fast. Many blocks. I could hardly keep up with her. She seemed very... enthusiastic. I think she must be off to elope or run away. I was so angry and so broken."

Broken. Elijah glanced at Hannah. He remembered feeling broken himself at that age. The moment Hannah had told him she'd accepted Peter's proposal.

"Finally I catch up to her," he continued, "and ask her what she is doing. I tell her she is stupid, acting like a child and should come home with me now."

The more Daniel talked, the more Hannah tensed. Elijah reached a hand over and touched her shoulder. "Are you sure you want to hear all of this?"

She nodded. "Yes. What did my daughter say?" She looked to Daniel.

"She told me to go home. That I was going to ruin everything. I asked, what can I ruin? She was ruining everything all by herself. But she says I don't know anything. That she is making a difference. Whatever that meant. Then she just keeps going. I followed her to a big apartment building. Outside, there are some boys, men really, mean-looking, bully-types. I am scared for her. But she goes through them like nothing. They say hi to her and let her pass. But it's not so easy for me.

"They stop me. They take my hat. They push me. Make me go on my knees. They are going to beat me. But Jessica returns and tells them not to waste time. She and another girl. This other girl tells them to walk me to the train and make sure I get on."

"Another girl?" Elijah asked.

"Yes, I think they called her Brit."

"Brittney Baker?"

"Yes. Maybe. I don't know. But she came out,

like I said, with Jessica. Then I was walked to the train and forced on by these boys."

"Did Jessica come home with you?"

He shook his head. "No. She didn't even go to the station. She stayed with her fancy friend."

"Did you ever see Jessica again?"

Daniel paused, looking from Hannah to him and back again to Hannah.

"We need to know the truth, Daniel. The more I know, the better I can help you…and Hannah." Eli tried to give an encouraging look to help the boy to trust him. "This isn't about you getting into trouble. This is about stopping a killer. You have to understand that."

Daniel still hesitated.

Hannah leaned forward and touched the boy's knee. "It's okay, Daniel. I know that you loved her. And she loved you, too. I don't blame you for following her."

A tear rolled down the boy's smooth cheek.

"When did you last see her?" Eli asked again.

"I did not see her again." Daniel stared at the floor, avoiding Eli's gaze.

Elijah sighed. The boy was lying or leaving something out. "But you went back to the city?"

Daniel lifted his eyes, then froze when they reached Elijah's gaze. "I did. I went back to the city after…after Jessica was found. I wanted to know who this friend was. Why Jessica had left me. Why I'd lost her." He dropped his head in his hands. "Jessica was gone—I couldn't ask her. And I had to know."

"What happened when you went back? Did you talk to Jessica's friend?"

He nodded, looking away. "Yes. She looked bad, this time. Not like before. There was a cut on her face. And she wouldn't tell me anything about Jessica or what had happened that night. And then those boys come again and they made me leave."

"They beat you up?"

"*Jah*. They said that if I didn't find this journal, I'd end up like Jessica. When I told them I didn't know where or what it was, they said to ask her mama. One of them held a gun to my head and pulled the trigger just to scare me."

"Is that who came here today?"

"I don't know. But I don't think so. Those boys they talk like kids, you know…"

"Street. They talk street."

"*Jah,* they talk street. Very hard to understand. But the men tonight. They sound older. Educated. Good English. Not street."

Elijah shook his head. Was this kid telling the truth? If so, this story painted a rather grim picture of Jessica—stealing, lying, involved with a gang.

He didn't know exactly what he'd expected to

find out about Jessica—perhaps that she'd been dragged into the city, forced somehow—certainly not that she'd taken a train there alone. Intentionally.

"Do you know the address of the apartments you went to when you followed her?"

"Kensington. From the train stop, it was three blocks west and two north. There was a restaurant across the street called the Imperial."

One of the worst parts of town. Elijah pulled his phone from his pocket.

"Pease don't tell the police about me," Daniel said. "Please."

Elijah could see the fear in the boy's eyes.

He walked to the corner of the room and called his partner. "More bad news here," he said to Tucci, catching him up on the case. "How about on your end?"

"It's pretty interesting, Miller," Tucci said. "I got the info on your symbol and on your girl. First of all, there are about twenty Brittney Bakers in Philadelphia, but only one with a record and between the ages of thirteen and twenty. So I figured that must be her."

"Got an address?"

"Yes," Tucci said, "4203 Yanger Street, number 502, across from the Imperial."

Then that part of Daniel's story was true. Yanger Street was exactly three blocks from the train at Broad. It was also the worst area of the city—the roughest and dirtiest. It was no place for a young girl and certainly no place for an Amish one. Elijah glanced back at Daniel and Hannah still sitting in the corner. Maybe the kid *was* telling the truth. But that prospect made his stomach churn for Hannah's sake. It was so important to her that she'd been a good mother, that she'd done all the right things, that Jessica had been a good girl. He knew this story of Daniel's must have been the hardest for her to hear.

"Why is she on record?"

"She's run away from home four times," Tucci said. "One time she was gone for a month. Got all the way to New York. She was working the streets."

Elijah rubbed his face. That was not anything he wanted to share with Hannah. "What's up with her home life? Why run?"

"There's not much there, only that she lives with the dad, who is really the second stepdad. No record of the actual father," Tucci said. "But this guy is acting guardian and get this—he is former D.C. Metro. His name is Jackson. Had some serious charges brought up against him three years ago, so he resigned from the force. He's been off the grid ever since. Supposedly, he's working as a security guard for Philadelphia Party Rentals Incorporated. I found a huge file on him, pictures included. I'm going to forward it to you."

"I don't have internet out here."

"Your BlackBerry, man."

He laughed. "I'll have to sit back out in my car and recharge. So, what about the symbol?"

"I'm getting to that. The symbol, turns out, is the marketing logo for a Fortune 500 company called Dutch Confidential. They own and operate a lot of business up and down the east coast, but mostly they work in electronic security systems. But guess what else they own? Philadelphia Party Rentals."

"The company that Brittney's stepdad works for as a security guard, right?"

"Right."

"Hmm. Why does a party rental operation need an ex-cop or security guard working there?"

"Exactly. I was wondering the same thing. So I called a friend of mine at Metro and he said this guy, Jackson, is slick—a dirty cop with big-time connections. Watch your back, Miller."

"Will do." Elijah folded the phone and put it back into his pocket. Slowly, he walked back to Hannah and Daniel, wondering what to do next. He could clean up the house. Get Abigail's buggy from the ditch before Thomas would be left to deal with it. Or he could tell Hannah that exactly what she feared most was true—that Jessica had befriended some pretty bad people.

Hannah wasn't sure what she thought of Daniel's story. It surprised her that Elijah had not called Chief McClendon to make a report, neither about the ransacked house nor about Daniel's participation in the whole affair. When Thomas and Nana returned, he solicited Daniel's help in pulling the broken buggy back to the barn and later in cleaning up the house.

Nana and Thomas remained quiet as they all worked to restore order to their home. It was late when Elijah drove Daniel home. Even later when he returned and they all went to bed.

Another short night and Hannah did not sleep well even knowing Elijah had camped out on their living room floor in order to watch all points of entry into the downstairs.

He was still sleeping when she descended to help with morning milking. She stopped and studied the angular cut of his jaw. A warm pang flashed through her belly. She leaned forward and replaced the quilt, which had fallen from his shoulders. Her fingers brushed over his tight chest.

"You do not need to help with milking, Hannah." Thomas stood at the bottom stair, rolling up the cuff of his sleeves. Disapproval in his eyes.

"Our nephew Samuel is coming. You could sleep another hour."

Hannah shrank away from Elijah. Once again she had hurt Thomas's feelings and looked ungrateful for all he had done for her. How he must loathe her and think her a reckless woman. Was she? She had always been so prudent in her actions, as a youth and as a woman. Had that changed? Had seeing Elijah again made her forget her place? She prayed it was not so but that she acted only in sisterly love for her old friend even though she knew that in this matter, her head and heart were not in agreement.

"You must be glad your money has been returned," she said, wondering what Thomas thought of last night's events. "Will you go to the elders with what the boy has done? And with the break-in?"

"I will not. This is Elijah's puzzle to solve. I want only that you are safe. If he sees no need for it, then I do not, either." He turned away, placing his straw hat over his long brown locks. "Anyway, the youth seemed punished enough in his fear. His involvement with my own niece forced his behavior. I cannot punish him for that. He will work the next two Saturdays with me in the fields. And I will welcome his help."

She bowed her head to him, then scurried to the kitchen and began to brew the tea and coffee.

"I am glad your money has been restored. You are a good steward."

"The money belongs to God." He corrected her praise, as such things were not to be said aloud. "Even when it is taken, it belongs to God. But since it is again in my care, I have an idea. We will purchase a new buggy for Abigail. And when you return from the city, she will take my dun-colored gelding. He is an easy fellow—a much better match for her than that young, green mare. We will keep the mare for training and return her smooth and steady in a year's time."

Hannah was not surprised by Thomas's generosity. He was a good man. She *was* surprised that he had approved the plan that she go into the city with Elijah and Abigail. Elijah must have spoken with him last night. She had not really agreed to go, and after the break-in and the story from Daniel, it did not seem the rational thing to do. "Thomas, I have no desire to go into the city. You must know that. I admit I wonder what Jessica had gotten involved in, but I am perfectly satisfied to let Elijah find those answers on his own. I have plenty to tend to here."

"I do not care for you to go to the city, either, Hannah, but I think perhaps you are safer with Elijah. I am not trained in the ways of the world as our friend is. I must trust you to him for the day. And I do trust him. It seems his intentions toward you and his motivations for being here are truly noble. I understand as well as any man wanting to prove that past choices were justified. Be careful." He tipped his hat to her. "I will take no breakfast this morning. Good day."

As he left through the kitchen door, Hannah struggled to comprehend Thomas's meaning. After she and Nana had retired, the two men had spoken of the day's events and apparently of other things as well, such as her. She must conclude from Thomas's attitude and Elijah's words the previous night that Elijah had no lingering feelings for her. He was only there to prove to all of Willow Trace that his profession was respectable. She should be relieved that her heart was therefore not in danger, but she was not. She was disappointed, but that would pass. Elijah would go home when this journal or whatever was found, and she would stay there. The realization left Hannah feeling more alone than ever before.

Elijah watched as Hannah, seated beside him in the Mustang, clung with one hand to her starched prayer *Kapp*. A serene smile fixed on her lips. He wasn't sure if she enjoyed the open-top ride into town, but she had asked for it and he had obliged her. An occasional laugh slipping from her lips as Abigail leaned forward between the two of them, recounting the details of her "date" with

Mr. Phelps. Although Elijah paid more attention to the way the sun sparkled over Hannah's porcelain skin. He studied the happy curve of her mouth. And when the wind would blow just the right way, her scent would tease him into wanting a taste of her lips and a touch of her hand.

Good thing he'd left Willow Trace when she married Peter. It would have been torturous being around her all the time with her married to someone else. It was hard enough being back there and even thinking about the fact that she would soon marry Thomas. Not that he didn't wish them well. He wanted Hannah to be happy and he obviously wasn't the man for that job. Didn't mean he loved her any less.

He'd been careful the night before to convince both Hannah and Thomas that he had no interest in a relationship beyond friendship with Hannah. But the truth was, he did. He missed home. He missed the Amish ways. He missed feeling that close to God all of the time. He missed Hannah.

But then there was his *Dat* who would never change his opinion. His father would never understand his calling to police work. He would never accept Eli back in Willow Trace. So there was no reason to even entertain the idea of making amends, much less bring it up with Hannah or his sister. Abigail would push him to come home, no doubt. But Hannah? She had tender feelings for him. That was clear. But she had always had those feelings and it didn't lead to anything before. Who was to say it would now? And if it didn't, could he take another rejection from the same woman? He wasn't willing to find out.

Once he knew Hannah would be safe again— that they *all* would be safe again—he would get as far away from Willow Trace as possible.

"So, no second outing with Mr. Phelps?" he teased his sister, trying to push his mind away from his own emotions.

"No. An old *Maidel* I am and always will be." Abigail laughed.

"And what about you, my brother? Have you never thought to take a wife?" she asked.

"No. I haven't really," he said. "I've been married to my job."

"That is a strange expression." Hannah turned to him. "Surely you do not mean that. In our spirit we should be married to Christ, no? Not our work."

Elijah swallowed hard. Hannah had misunderstood and his words had disappointed her. "Yes. It's a strange expression. I just meant that I spend more time working than I do courting."

"Oh, I see." That seemed to relieve her somewhat, but she still seemed a bit displeased. "But you used to want a family so badly. Is this not a desire of yours any longer?"

He wanted a family with *her* so badly. But he would not say that aloud, as she had chosen to have a family with someone else. "We want many things when we are young. But our paths don't always take us where we think they will," he said instead.

Hannah's face washed over with sadness. Of course, her path had brought her many losses. He should have been more careful of his words. He hadn't meant to upset her.

Abigail leaned up between them. "That's what makes life so exciting. You never know which way your path will go next. Who knows? God could have new spouses for us all."

Hannah didn't comment. She seemed to suddenly realize she was in the heart of downtown Philly.

"I'm sorry your first trip into the city is to this part of town," Elijah said to her.

"I only want to find out about Jessica," she answered.

"Are you sure this is the right address?" Abigail asked.

"Yes, this is the place." Elijah indicated a large high-rise apartment on the corner. He circled the block until he found a spot to parallel-park his car against the curb. "This neighborhood is worse than I remembered. Maybe you ladies would like to stay in the car? Abs, you remember how to drive, right?"

"No way. I wouldn't drive in all this traffic for anything. I'll take my chances on the street."

"Me, too." Hannah nodded, though he could see she was filled with fear. "I've come this far. I might as well meet this friend of Jessica's."

Eli nodded. He closed up the car and led the ladies to the front of the building. A group of young men appeared as they turned the corner. There were six of them, all wearing caps, chains and jeans so large they fell halfway down their thighs. Elijah could only assume it was the same welcoming gang that had escorted Daniel to the train.

When they saw that the three of them wanted to enter the building, they formed a barricade in front of the door.

"Can we help you?" one of them asked.

Elijah put the ladies behind him, standing like a wall in front of the gang of young men. "We're not here to make trouble. We're on a social call."

"A social call, huh?" the kid continued. "Perfect. 'Cause we are the social committee. Welcome to the hood."

Another young man in the group stepped forward. "Hey, guys, they dress like that other girl—remember? That girl with Britt?"

Elijah tried to remain calm. "You know an Amish girl?"

"We know everybody. Amish. Polish. Italian. It's our job."

"Yeah, it's our job to know everyone...especially the ladies."

"And these ladies are fine." One of the gang circled around and came close to both Hannah and Abigail. He reached out and touched Hannah's bare neck. She flinched, and lowered her eyes to the ground.

"Even under all that dress. Can't hide what looks fine," said another boy, joining his friend.

"Mmm-hmm," they hummed together. The two largest boys stepped between Elijah and the two women. Elijah was wishing he'd brought Tucci with them. At least then he would not feel so outnumbered and unable to protect both his sister and Hannah.

In any case, he did not want to fight with these hooligans in case they had any information about Jessica and the night she was killed. Possibly even they were the killers as Daniel had suggested. However, seeing them in person, he doubted that. He knew the type—at this age, they liked to throw their weight around, but they were mostly talk. They certainly didn't have the discipline yet to rise to any kind of high level within a gang. And that made him wonder if any information they had was worth subjecting Hannah and his sister to their rough language and crudeness.

He looked back to Hannah. "Let's just get inside. We can talk to them later if we need to," he whispered.

But the group had circled around them. They laughed and continued to make offensive suggestions.

"That's enough, guys," Elijah said. "Let the ladies pass. We have someone to talk to."

"You married to these girls?" one of them snarled. He reached out and touched the strings of Hannah's prayer *Kapp*.

"Who cares if I am or I ain't?" Elijah let his cop street training fall into practice. "I said to let the ladies pass or I'll—"

The most aggressive of the group pushed Elijah at the shoulder, knocking him back into the boys behind, who stiff-armed him, shoving him back forward. "Or you'll what, Blondie? We ain't afraid of you."

"You're assaulting a police officer," Abigail announced. "I'm a witness. How about you, Mrs. Nolt? Are you a witness?"

Hannah nodded, while Elijah reached into his coat.

"That true? You a cop?" one kid said. The others backed away.

Elijah pulled his ID card from his pocket and showed the boys.

"You Philadelphia P.D.?" the leader asked.

"That's what the card says, doesn't it?"

"I ain't never seen you on this street."

"I'm I.A."

"You don't look like no cop," he said.

"Look like one of those guys in a BVD ad," another said. The others laughed and snorted.

"Why are you here?" the leader said. "Nothing funny goes down on this block. You would know that if you were really Philly P.D."

"Like nothing funny happened here when an Amish girl came to visit, then returned home murdered?" Elijah asked.

The boys moved away faster. "Hey, we was just kidding. We don't know any Amish. We don't know what you talking 'bout, man."

"Tell me about Brittney Baker," Elijah said.

"What's there to tell?" one boy answered. "She lives here. We don't talk to her much. She's quiet, you know."

"That's not what we heard. We heard you are good friends and that you do anything she asks."

"Look, man, no one touches Brit. Her dad's..." He looked around to his friends, who had backed up even farther.

"Her dad is what?" Elijah pushed.

The kid eyed Hannah and Abigail, took a step

backward and shrugged. Then he turned and hightailed it away from them as fast as possible, catching up to his buddies already a block away.

TWELVE

Hannah looked over at Eli. "Are you okay?"

"More like are *you* okay?" Eli gave her a cock-eyed smile. "I'm fine. But I am anxious to get going. We need to get to Brittney before she and her father hear that we're coming. Are you two able to handle that? Or was this too much already?"

"We are fine. Maybe not used to being eyed like animals for the purchase. But fine," Abigail answered.

"I will be fine." Hannah nodded. "This is why you did not tell them you were a police officer? Because they will bring more trouble? Do you not think that they—that they…"

"Killed Jessica?"

"No. I don't think they are killers. Not yet. They are just the lookout. Brittney's father must have some power over them. I'd guess they are on their way right now to warn him that we are here."

They entered the building and took an elevator

to the fifth floor. The apartments had a strange odor, although the interior proved to be much nicer than what the outside had first promised. The paint was clean. The woodwork and carpets were fancy and colorful.

Elijah knocked at door 502. He held his little card to a small glass hole in the center of the door and announced himself as Detective Miller of the Philadelphia Police Department. The door creaked open though it was still connected to the wall by a link chain, as if someone expected a person to knock and then come bursting into the house. These English were most strange. She didn't know how Elijah had made his way among them for so many years.

"My stepfather isn't…" The dark-headed girl at the door stopped speaking as her eyes fell on Hannah and Abigail and their clothing.

Through the tiny slit of a doorway, Hannah could tell the girl was thin and tall. And very pretty. Much like the dark looks of her girl Jessica. Most certainly they were close in age. Was this girl the reason for Jessica's death? Hannah bit her lip, trying to shut out the wild surge of desperate emotions that filled her heart.

"Not here to see anyone's father. We're here to see Brittney Baker," Elijah said. "Are you Brittney Baker?"

The girl was wide-eyed. "Why do you need to talk to Brittney Baker?"

"We understand that she's friends with a girl named Jessica Nolt. We have some questions for her."

The girl seemed to consider his words for a few seconds, and then the door closed fast. Hannah heard the metal of the chain slinking behind the door, and then the girl opened it again, completely, and bade them enter, but only into the foyer.

"I haven't seen Jessica in a week." She stared at Hannah. "Are you her mom? She said her mom was young and had green eyes."

"Are you Brittney Baker?" Elijah asked before Hannah could reply.

"Yeah, I'm Brittney." She shuffled her weight from side to side and pulled the small, short jacket tight around her shoulders. "So what?"

"Can we ask you a few questions about Jessica? It won't take long."

She nodded, albeit reluctantly.

"Tell us about the last time you saw her," Elijah said.

Again, she looked at Hannah. "This isn't going to get her in trouble, is it?"

"No," Elijah assured her. "You aren't going to get Jessica in trouble."

"Then…why do you need to know about her?"

She folded her arms across her chest. "Cops only come around asking questions when someone's gonna get in trouble. I don't have to answer any questions."

"No, you don't have to answer any questions. But we are hoping you will. This is Jessica's step-mother. She came a long way to meet you and find out what happened to her daughter."

Hannah gave the girl a pleading look and nodded. "Please. I want to know what happened to my daughter."

Brittney's defiant expression changed to one of concern. "What do you mean what happened to her? She came by and we hung out a couple of times. No big deal, right? She told me she was on *rum-spring* or something which meant that it was okay for her to hang out."

"Did you see Jessica last Monday?" Elijah said.

Brittney looked down as if recalling a bad memory and nodded gently.

"Please. Please tell us what you know. It's important." Hannah came forward, placing her hands on the girl's forearm. Brittney retracted as if Hannah's touch were fire.

"What's wrong with your arms?" Abigail interrupted. "You stand like you have pain. You are hurt, aren't you? That's why you're holding that jacket around your shoulders. Brother, I have seen this before with some of my patients."

"No, I'm fine." Brittney backed away. "I just don't like anyone touching me."

Elijah shot his sister a look, which Hannah supposed meant Abby should leave that alone. And Hannah, despite her overwhelming desire to put this behind her and go back home to normalcy, could not help her worry and disappointment.

Elijah turned back to Brittney. "So, you girls hung out a lot?"

"Yes, I guess. She was cool." Brittney stopped and looked at each of them. "So, is she missing or something?"

Hannah wondered that Elijah did not tell her that Jessica was gone.

"Do you know anything about a journal that Jessica had?"

"Oh, man." Brittney shivered and backed away from them. Her eyes darted between the faces of the adults. "My dad sent you here, didn't he? He's so mad about that stupid journal. Look, I don't know where she took it. Okay? Just go. Get out of here."

"Your dad didn't send us here," Elijah said. "We got your name from some of Jessica's friends in Willow Trace and we're here to find out what you and she did last Monday night. Where did you go? Who did you see and talk to? Can you help us out or not?"

She turned her back to them, holding herself as if she were cold. "I want to talk to Jessica first."

"I'm sorry, you can't do that," Elijah said. Hannah could tell now that the poor girl was starting to cry.

"Yeah, why not?" she asked.

"Because she's dead," Elijah said quietly.

Brittney turned back. Her face went pale and her eyes widened. She held a hand to her mouth as if she might get sick. Curses slipped from her lips, then regrets, and a single tear spilled over her cheek. She hurried to the window and looked out. "You should go."

"Because of your friends downstairs?" Elijah asked. "Did they hurt Jessica? Did they hurt *you?*"

"You'd better go," Brittney said. "For all our sakes, just go." She started shooing them toward the front door.

"You won't tell us what happened?" Abigail said.

"I don't know what happened. Really. And I'm really sorry about Jessica. I am. But go. Before it's too late. Go. And don't come back." She herded them out into the hallway.

Hannah felt she did not need any encouragement. She was quite ready to leave this place. But Abigail hovered at the doorway and pulled a slip of paper from her apron. She handed the card to Brittney.

"What's this?"

"My address," Abigail said. "I'm a nurse. Someone should look at your injuries."

Brittney took the card, then slammed the door behind her. The sound of the metal chain sliding closed rang through the long hallway.

"I don't think she had anything to do with Jessica's death," Elijah said.

"How can you tell?" Abigail asked.

"Her body language. Her expressions."

"Then why did she seem so scared? Is she afraid of those boys? Daniel made it sound like they listened to everything she said."

"She wasn't so scared until we brought up the journal," Elijah said.

"And that made her think of her *Dat,*" Hannah added.

"You would make a good detective, Hannah." Elijah gave her a nod. "Exactly. She's afraid of her dad and that journal. Looks more and more like Daniel's story was the truth. If only she could tell us what's in that journal, or what happened the last time she saw Jessica, but I don't think she'll talk unless we get her out of this place, and that's not going to happen with the friendly neighborhood watch downstairs."

Hannah knew Elijah was talking about the repulsive young men that had surrounded them. She slumped and broke into tears. "I can't believe my girl came to this horrible place. What was she thinking? Why did she tell Daniel that she was doing something good? What good is there to do here?"

Abigail put her arm around Hannah. "There, now. We may never know what she was about. But God does and He is a loving, kind, forgiving God. Do not fret, my sister. Jessica is safe now and in the hands of her Maker. She was a good girl. We will never think of her any other way."

Hannah wished she could feel so sure. She wished she could push the ugly words of her neighbors out of her head. But she feared when news of Jessica's visits to the city spread through Willow Trace—and word would spread—the talk about Jessica and her poor parenting skills and weak faith would only increase. Not that she cared so much what others thought. She did not. What bothered her was the doubt in her own heart that she had been a good mother. What bothered her was the inner fear that others spoke the truth. Otherwise, how could she have let this happen?

Elijah was thankful that Abigail was there to soften this experience for Hannah. It was rough even for him to imagine a sheltered Amish teen in such a setting. And Jessica had definitely been there. Brittney even seemed protective of her. Eli wasn't sure if that was a good thing or a bad thing. And only God knew what Jessica had been up to in such a place. Elijah had a hard time believing that Jessica's visit had been of an innocent nature—not in this part of town.

Drugs and prostitution certainly came to mind. Poor Hannah. If she weren't clearly in imminent danger, he'd have to agree with Thomas that all this searching for answers over Jessica's death was a bad idea.

He stopped in front of the elevator and pushed the call button.

"I'd prefer the stairs," Hannah said weakly.

Elijah nodded. Of course, Hannah didn't want to ride in an elevator. He should have thought of that himself. With a sigh, he made a move toward the stairwell, but at the same time the elevator door opened.

Abigail grabbed Hannah's hand and pulled her into the lift. "Oh, come on. It's probably the only day you ever will travel on an elevator. Once more. Trust me, it's better than walking down so many flights of stairs."

Elijah entered after them. A sinking feeling in his stomach made him wish they had listened to Hannah and taken the stairs.

"What's the matter, Eli?" Abigail studied his face.

"Nothing." He turned and tried to smile. No need to worry the ladies. They were nervous enough after the encounter with the gang and the not-so-wonderful conversation with Jessica's friend, Miss Brittney Baker. What he wished he had time to do was comb the neighborhood further in order to gather more information about the type of friendship that had existed between the Amish girl and the city one. But he couldn't do that today. For one, it was already out that he was a cop. More than likely that meant that no one in the neighborhood would talk to him. And more important, he could not imagine exposing poor Hannah to any more of downtown Philadelphia. She looked ready to faint as it was.

He tried to give her a reassuring smile as the doors opened behind him to exit the elevator. But instead of Abigail and Hannah smiling back at him, their eyes widened and they backed away from him.

"Watch out!" Abigail squealed.

Dread flowed through Elijah and he anticipated an attack from behind.

Elijah didn't even get a chance to turn his head. A strong force struck him in the back of the head. His knees gave way and he fell like a bag of rocks to the floor. Everything went black.

THIRTEEN

"Wake up! He's got Hannah!" Abigail's words came to him in pieces like a bad phone connection. His head and neck ached. Two hands pulled at his shoulders. Elijah rolled onto his back and forced his eyes open. Abigail stood over him with a frantic expression.

"Get up!" she said.

"What—what happened?" He put a hand to his head and with the other pushed up to a sitting position. It was then he remembered vaguely the scene in the elevator. Someone had been behind him. Someone large and strong. He'd been struck in the back of the head.

"It was terrible, it was. He came so fast. Hit you in the head. Took Hannah. I tried to stop him, brother, but he swatted me away like a fly, he did." Abigail grabbed hold of his hand and tried her best to help him to his feet.

"What do you mean, he's got Hannah?" Elijah balanced his weight over his two feet. His head felt like an anvil and throbbed with nearly debilitating pain. He lifted a hand to his aching cranium. Warm blood stuck to his fingers. He'd been struck with something blunt like the back end of a gun. "Who has Hannah?"

"I don't know," she said. "The man was tall and thin with reddish-blond hair. I've never seen him before. He was so fast, I tell you. Put you down and took Hannah in one motion. He had a gun."

Reddish-blond hair. *Tall. Strong.* Eli had seen photos in the file his partner, Tucci, had forwarded him the night before. The description sounded just like Flynn Jackson, Brittney's stepdad. Jackson must have heard from the front door gang of their arrival. But if they worked for Jackson and also did whatever Jessica and Brittney requested, that painted a strange picture—and not one too favorable for Jessica.

As these thoughts raced through one side of his aching head, the other could think of nothing but Hannah. "Which way did he take her?"

"I do not know. Maybe this way." Abigail pointed away from the building entrance and toward the back of the first-floor hallway.

The stairwell, maybe? Or he could have taken her out the back. Eli's heart sank. He had no idea.

"How long was I out?"

"Not long, brother. The elevator doors, they close and then they open again. Two times."

That was not too long. But, still, they had a head start and he wasn't even sure which way to begin looking. His chances of finding them by himself were too few.

He limped out of the elevator, pulling his keys and cell phone from his pocket. He dialed Tucci.

"I need backup. Hannah's been abducted. Possibly by Jackson. He's armed."

"Location?"

"The address you gave me yesterday."

"Roger, that," Tucci answered. "Be there in ten."

"Bring a team."

"Already on it, Miller. And wait for us. No Rambo moves, Amish boy."

Elijah clicked off and handed his keys to Abigail. "Run to my car. Lock yourself in and stay hidden. If you have to, drive away. I know you remember from your *Rumspringa*."

She reached for the keys but hesitated. "You can hardly stand, Elijah. Shouldn't I stay and—"

"Go," he ordered her. His voice sounded weak and stressed. No wonder she didn't want to leave him. "I don't want to be distracted by worrying about you, too, Abby. Just go. That is the most helpful thing you can do."

Abigail took the keys and ran from the building. Elijah prayed she would make it to his car safely. What had he done by bringing them there? It had escalated things—that was for sure. Now he only hoped that he could get Hannah back safely and then make this terrible incident work in their favor.

Elijah looked in every direction. Which way would he go with a hostage? Maybe to a place he knew well. Like home. Sure. That was a good place to start. Back at Jackson's apartment.

Elijah ran toward the door to the stairs, ignoring the shooting pain in his head. Pulling his gun from his jacket, he slipped into the spiraling stairwell. *Please, Lord, lead me to them. Keep Hannah calm and safe.*

With a quick move, he aimed his Glock upward and stepped into the center of the stairwell, looking both up and then down. Twelve stories of stairs. No basement access. That meant there was another set of stairs. What if he'd picked the wrong ones? How could he know? And not a puff of air stirred. One or two minutes were like an eternity to be behind in a chase. Too much time had passed since Jackson had attacked him and made off with Hannah.

Pushing his discouraging thoughts away again, Elijah hurtled up the stairs, his adrenaline helping to numb the pain in his head. At the top of the fifth flight, he plowed through the stairwell door and raced down the hallway. He knocked hard at the door to 502.

"Flynn Jackson, open up! Philadelphia P.D."

From inside, Elijah heard a loud *click* that sounded all too familiar—the lock and load of a shotgun. *Please let Hannah be safe,* he prayed as he dove out of the way of the door.

He hit the floor to the left side of the door and rolled onto his shoulder. A terrific blast blew through the front door of the apartment. Definitely a shotgun. No wonder his head hurt if he'd been hit in the head with the back end of one of those.

Eli protected his face from the flying debris. Then he sat up and aimed his Glock at the hole in the door, ready for Jackson to peek through the destruction.

But no one moved. From inside sounded Jackson's low grumbles, a woman's cries and furniture scooting across or toppling to the floor.

"Hannah?" Elijah hurried to get up and pressed his back to the wall next to the blown-out front door.

"Elijah!" Hannah cried from within. Terror sounded in her voice.

He had to save her. But alone? Jackson could blow him away with one step inside the apartment. But to wait five to ten more minutes for his backup? Was he willing to risk that? To wait?

"Send the woman out, or I'm coming in," he said. He cocked his gun so Jackson would know he was armed. "It's over, Jackson. I called backup. You got nowhere to go. A SWAT team will be here in no time."

"How's your head, Miller?" he yelled back with a laugh. "Seems like I'm always looking at the back of it, don't it?"

"And seems like you're always hiding, Jackson…in the trees, outside the elevator, in a stable, on the side of a road…from the Metro police." Elijah leaned to the side and looked through the front door. He saw nothing. Jackson and Hannah were nowhere near the entry.

"You don't know anything about me, Amish boy. But I know everything about you—you and your pretty girlfriend here. I think she likes me. And what do I care if you come in? You are out there all by yourself. Now, if you Plain folk would just give me what I need, I will let her go. But not until I have it in my hands."

"No one has anything of yours." Elijah slid into the entrance hall. From there he spotted Jackson in a mirror. He dropped low to stay out of sight. Jackson reloaded the shotgun with one hand. With the other, he forced Hannah against his chest, holding her by a fistful of her luxurious hair. "Let her go."

"No can do. The little Amish girl said her *Mamm* knew where to find the journal. And this is her *Mamm*. You should be thankful I found you before any of the other interested parties. They'd just cut both your throats like they did that troublemaking Jessica."

Elijah slid farther into the apartment. "Hold it, Jackson. Put the weapon down. I have a clear shot."

Jackson tossed the gun at him. When it hit the ground, it fired at the wall, blasting shrapnel into the long hallway. Elijah covered his face and had to back away.

Jackson let out a low, husky chuckle. "How's your shot now, Amish boy?"

"Let her go, Jackson. She doesn't know where the journal is," Elijah repeated. "I'll turn my head and let you run. A favor from one cop to another. Do it now before my team gets here."

"Thanks, but I really need that journal. Bring it to me and then you can have her back."

Elijah scooted back into the hallway and across from the mirror. Not only had Jackson moved close to a back door and window leading onto a fire escape, but he had another gun in his hand. This one a small pistol aimed right at Hannah's head. Even from that distance, he could see the huge gold ring on his third finger, sporting the symbol of Dutch Confidential. No mistaking, this was the tall, fair-skinned man from his cousin's farm, also Brittney's stepfather.

Hannah had her eyes closed tight with tears on her cheeks.

Where was his team? Where was his backup? Elijah had to rush forward and save Hannah. He had to because if he lost Hannah, he'd lose everything.

Protect Elijah, Lord. Protect me. Deliver us from this place. Hannah kept her eyes closed and tried to be *absent from the body and present with the Lord.*

"Let her go." Elijah's voice sounded in the foyer. *Thank You, Lord. Thank You for sparing him.* God had sent Elijah to help her. Just hearing his voice made her feel better. She hadn't been able to see him yet, but she could hear him, first through the door, and then from inside the apartment. The man holding her had shot his horrible weapon twice. Each time Hannah feared he'd harmed or killed Elijah. But then she'd hear his voice again, as strong as ever.

The horrible man dragged her by the hair. Her neck felt as if it might snap from her head. Even with her eyes closed, she could feel the barrel of his gun pointed into her temple.

"Let her go," Elijah said again. He sounded calm but authoritative. It reminded Hannah of the way the elders spoke when making a ruling no one in the *Ordnung* was to question.

But the redheaded man did not let her go. Instead, he tightened his grip, digging his fingertips into her scalp. Agony pealed through her body. Each time he turned, each time he moved, the pain increased. How could a human treat another human so?

Give me strength, Lord.

"She doesn't have what you want." This time he spoke, Elijah came boldly into the room. At the sound of his voice, her eyes flew open. His gun pointed straight ahead. "Now let her go and I'll let you go."

The man yanked Hannah placing her directly in front of him like a shield. He laughed. So close to her she could feel his breath.

"Elijah! Please!" She could not stop her tears as he pressed the cold end of the gun harder into her head. The trigger clicked in her ear and she trembled. Her weight, ironically, was held up by the hair on her head.

"He can't help you, lady. He wouldn't pull that trigger and risk hitting you. Actually, I don't know if he could even pull that trigger. He is Amish, after all. You're just going to have to tell me where my journal is," he said.

"I do not know," she cried. "I do not know."

"Let her go." Brittney appeared in the corner of the large living space.

"What are you doing here? You should be at school." He sounded truly surprised.

"Drop your weapon." Elijah had moved closer. Behind him several other officers filed into the apartment.

Jackson cursed. "No. And if you want to keep this lady alive, you'll back out of here. Brittney, you, too, get out of here."

"Just let her go." Brittney moved closer. "If she knew where it was, she'd tell you."

The police ordered Brittney to step back. Instead she moved closer and once she was in reaching distance, Jackson grabbed hold of the girl, after shoving Hannah as hard as he could to the other side of the room.

She stumbled out of control toward Elijah and the others, blocking any access to Jackson or Brittney.

Elijah lowered his gun and scrambled toward her to help her up and out of harm's way.

"It's okay now. You're safe," he told her.

Shock distorted her reality. Hannah could barely register the words he spoke. She could barely feel his tender touch leading her from the apartment. She could still feel that hand in her hair yanking at her scalp.

"Did he hurt you badly?" Elijah's voice was a whisper compared to the commotion behind them.

"The building is surrounded," she heard one of

the other officers say. "Let the girl go and come with us."

"Not today, boys," the man replied.

Although he sounded less sure of himself, when Hannah looked over her shoulder she shuddered. Jackson had grabbed his stepdaughter around the waist and positioned her in front of him, just as he had held her seconds ago. But instead of controlling the girl with a handful of hair, he held a knife to her throat.

Hannah froze in the doorway watching as the knife pressed against Brittney's soft skin. The policemen didn't press toward Jackson, but stopped short, lowering their weapons. No one doubted he would hurt the child.

Oh, Lord, please, not another child.

"Elijah, please, can we not do something more?"

FOURTEEN

I can pray, Elijah thought to himself as he tried to move Hannah from the apartment. She wouldn't budge. She was as still and heavy as a sack of stones staring back at that girl. And how could she not be? The sight before her was one that would never fade from her mind. As it would never fade from his.

Jackson's ring and the blade of his knife flashed under the poor girl's chin.

"You got nowhere to go, Jackson," Tucci yelled from beside Eli. His partner and three SWAT team members had positioned themselves around the room—each with a rifle pointed at Jackson.

"Put the guns down." Jackson's voice made Eli's skin crawl.

Slowly, they lowered their guns to the floor.

"You're cornered," Tucci said.

Jackson smirked before pulling Brittney along with him as he slowly slinked to the back of the room where a single window was cracked open.

Jackson bent his knees and reached down, lifting the window wide. Then he backed through the open space like a panther onto the fire escape. The whole while he kept his stepdaughter as a shield with the knife to her neck. He dragged Brittney with him, then slammed the window closed and jammed it with the knife.

"No, Elijah. Why do they not stop him?" Hannah sounded hysterical, clutching on to him with a deathlike grip.

"We can't risk Brittney's life to get him, Hannah," he said to her. "But don't worry. We will catch up with him yet."

At last, she relaxed her frozen stance and he was able to pull her away.

She cried and shook against him. He held her close, supporting her and helping her out of the building. An emergency team rushed to them as they exited the building. A couple of EMTs whisked Hannah away from him to check her over for injuries. Other police hurried over to him.

"Tucci just radioed down. Jackson has vanished," they said. "The girl, too."

Elijah felt a surge of frustration and disappointment, but his thoughts remained mostly focused on Hannah.

Seated at the edge of the emergency truck, a worker handed her a blanket. She tried to smooth and tuck her loose hair. Her apron was smudged.

Her frock was ripped at the shoulder. She looked pale. Shaken. Exhausted.

He'd almost lost her. Again.

Thank You, Lord. Thank You for getting her out of there. He lifted the prayer and tried to release the fear that gripped him.

And the guilt. If something had happened to Hannah...

An EMT appeared before him. "The lady says you have a head injury?"

"I'm fine." Elijah stood suddenly, and homed in on Hannah. He had to hold her. He had to feel her in his arms and know that she was safe. That she was still alive.

In a second, he stood before her. He touched his hand gently to her smudged cheek. "I can't lose you, Hannah," he whispered. "I can't lose you again."

Then he lifted her into his arms and held her tighter than he'd ever held anyone.

"I can't lose you again."

Jackson and his stepdaughter were not caught. Mr. Tucci and Elijah's colleagues from the Philadelphia Police Department had come up empty-handed after a complete search of the building. It was as if Jackson and Brittney had vanished into thin air.

For a long time, Elijah, Abigail and Hannah

had to answer questions for the team of police. The EMTs strongly recommended a trip to the hospital, but Elijah seemed to know that Hannah couldn't take any more of the city.

She tried to focus on the fact that she and Elijah and Abigail were blessed to be alive. And she was so thankful for that. So very thankful. But she had seen and heard such atrocities that day and her mind could not leave the idea that her Jessica had seen and heard it all, as well. Maybe worse. She was starting to think that the gossips back in Willow Trace had been right to speculate about her daughter. Maybe Jessica's heart had not been so pure. The girl had certainly been spending time with terrible people. Today's trip into the city and the discovery of Jessica's secret life had made Hannah feel cheated and deceived. She was ashamed that she'd not been a better mother and prevented this. If she had, Jessica would still be alive. And Elijah wouldn't be there, making her confused and feeling so many things. Right now all she wanted to do was to collapse in a fit of tears until she washed away all the filth of the outside world.

Surely, some quiet prayer and hard work would set her right—no more thoughts about how she should have done things. No more thoughts about Elijah and the past...or the future. No more thoughts of how he'd held her in his arms.

"Do you think your partner and his team will find Jackson and Brittney?" Abigail asked from the seat behind her.

Hannah looked away and stared out the window at the rolling green hills. She didn't want to hear any more talk of Flynn Jackson or Brittney Baker or even of Jessica.

"I hope so," Elijah said. "I think if we can get Jackson into the station, we will be able to get the information we need. What exactly this journal is that he wants. And why he thinks Hannah has it. Tucci will also talk to people in the neighborhood and see what he can find out. Jackson said he wasn't the only one looking for the missing journal. I think that worries me most."

"You mean like those young men, who were so awful when we first arrived?" Abigail asked.

Hannah shuddered at the reminder.

"No. I think the gang is linked somehow, but remember Daniel said that they were friendly to Jessica and Brittney. That they even took him to the train station when Jessica asked them. I think Jackson is into things with much higher stakes than those kids on the street."

"Higher stakes?" Abigail asked.

"Yes. I think this journal must have some pretty serious information in it. Something that could hurt a lot of people. Maybe even get them killed or incarcerated."

"But why? Why would Jessica…" Hannah could not make sense of it all. How could her girl have gotten involved in such schemes?

Elijah reached over and held her hand. He was so strong. She could feel the power and strength flowing in him.

"My strength comes from the Lord," he said.

Hannah turned to him. "I understand better now what it is that you do."

He nodded. "Yes, thank you. I wish my *Dat* could see it, too."

Abigail smiled. "Give him time. He will see that you try to bring some order to the world."

"I didn't bring much order today." He frowned. "I nearly got us all killed…"

Abigail nodded. "Well, we are here to help. Even though I know it is hard." She patted Hannah's shoulder. "I think we must find this journal."

"Or at least figure out what information is in it," Elijah said.

"Ah. I can see in your eye you have an idea." Abigail grinned. "What is it? If we all think hard, maybe we can figure this out."

"I don't really know anything," Elijah said. "Just that Jackson was a dirty cop. He did and could still have access to all kinds of things."

"Dirty cop?" Hannah asked. "What does this mean?"

"It means he did police work and carried a

badge, but at the same time he took money from criminals by overlooking their crimes and helping them get away. Maybe making evidence disappear. Or selling secret information. Jackson is no longer a cop, but the rest of what he does could be the same. He could use old contacts inside the police department to get information, to get inside the system, to help bad people make money so that he can make money."

"But why would anyone in the police department work with such a man?" Abigail asked.

Elijah tilted his head. "Because, sadly, there are some cops on the force who want money more than they want to do what is right. And if they're greedy just once and agree to do one thing, then Jackson has a way to end their career and can blackmail them into doing more work for him. They don't want to lose their jobs. Trust me. I work Internal Affairs. This happens more than you really want to know."

"What a terrible man is this Flynn Jackson," Abigail said.

Hannah had tried not to listen, but no matter how much she wanted to block everything out, she could not. More than ever, right or wrong, she wanted to learn the truth. Without the whole truth, she might never accept that Jessica had turned out to be a bad girl. And she had to accept what had happened. She had to accept God's will.

Elijah had been right about that. He had been right about a lot of things. She turned to him. "Do you think he killed Jessica?"

Elijah turned to her. Regret shone out of his blue eyes. "I don't know. He said that someone else wanted the journal. He made it sound as if that person harmed your daughter and not him. But the way he grabbed Brittney with that knife... he certainly seemed capable of it."

Hannah put a hand to her stomach. She felt ill. She wondered how a mother could leave her child with such a man. But who was she to judge? She'd done no better with Jessica.

"Brittney could be lying, Hannah," Elijah said as if reading her thoughts. "Jessica might not have taken this journal. Maybe Brittney told Jackson this just to save her own skin."

His words were meant to comfort her, but they did not. She could only think of her own failing.

"So, what we really need," Abigail said, "is to find out what the journal actually is and what information it holds?"

"Yes," he answered. "And as hard as it is, we should start looking for it in Willow Trace."

"So you *do* think she took it?" Hannah asked.

"It doesn't matter what I think. *They* think she took it and they think *you* have it.... I just wish I knew better what I was looking for."

Hannah did not follow. "What do you mean? It's a journal, right?"

"I'm not sure that they mean an actual journal. Not like what you are thinking, a book with someone's personal thoughts in it."

"Then what?" Abigail asked.

"Okay. I just thought of this, but it makes sense. So, there's this retired guy I know from the Philly P.D., Mike. Mike works in security now on the weekends to earn a few bucks. He's at the downtown courthouse. Really tight security. Very high-tech systems. And Jackson supposedly works in security, too."

"And what?" she and Abigail asked at the same time.

"Well, all of this security is controlled by bar codes and card swiping. Mike said they are constantly changing the cards and the codes. And in case there's some sort of blackout or computer malfunction, the security people keep all these codes on a special storage device. It's changed out each week and synched with the mainframe system. For lack of a better word, they call this device the journal."

"Would having it be worth killing over?" Abigail asked.

"Sure. If a place has that kind of security, there must be something inside worth guarding."

"But Jessica? Taking something like this? Hiding it? Why?" Hannah closed her eyes and sighed, her stomach still churning. She didn't want to talk about any of these horrible things her daughter had gotten involved in.

"*If* she even took it, Hannah," he corrected her. "And I think when we know the answer to that question, we'll know the whole of this."

But would they? Hannah wondered.

No one spoke as they pulled back in front of Nolt Cottage. Thomas stood waiting. He'd replaced the broken window, making his stone cottage look as homey as ever. A brand-new carriage, and the gelding Thomas had spoken of earlier was tied to the hitching post. What a good man Thomas was. She should love him and want to marry him, but in her heart she knew she could not.

Strange emotions swept through her as she exited the car. She could not lift her head to Thomas. She could not look back to Elijah. The heaviness of the day weighed down on her. The loss of Jessica and Peter gripped her so tightly she felt as if she would snap. No hope for her future.

She rushed up the front porch steps and into the house. She would not love again. She could not risk the pain of losing anything else.

Elijah didn't think he could feel any worse than he already did. But when Hannah ran into the house, his heart ached ten times more than his head. He should never have taken her to Philadelphia. He'd thought it would help make Jessica's so-called friend feel comfortable and talk. And perhaps that connection did help somewhat, but it hadn't been worth the dangers that they'd all been exposed to. He'd always believed that seeking the truth was worth any risk, but that was only because he had never risked something he loved as much as Hannah.

He'd always thought that going home would turn his people further against him and make him feel even more alienated from the world he had grown up in. That was what he had feared—well, that and his *Dat*'s disapproval. He'd been right about his *Dat*. But he had been very wrong about his own experience. Instead of feeling alienated from the Amish, Elijah was finding that their beliefs and rules and laws made more sense to him than they ever had before. For the first time in a long while, he started to wonder what it would be like to come home for good. Lead a Plain life. The thought was very tempting—but also very distracting. He was getting too attached, too emotionally involved, and it was keeping him from solving the case. He wasn't doing a good job as a detective—and if he couldn't do that, then there was no reason for him to stay. No reason other than his love for Hannah, which seemed to grow stronger—and more hopeless—every day.

She'd made her choice long ago, and it was long past time for him to accept it. But accepting it meant he needed to go. It had been easy to leave before when Hannah hadn't wanted him, when his father had challenged him. Leaving this time would not be easy at all, but it was exactly what he needed to do and he needed to do it now.

Elijah kicked a stone in the path, watching Thomas go in after Hannah. That was another reason to leave. He needed to get over that feeling of jealousy and be able to wish Thomas and Hannah well. They would be good together. And he had no doubt that Thomas cared for her. He turned to his sister.

"I need to have my captain send someone else here to protect Hannah. I should never have come back home. I've only made things worse."

Abigail frowned. "You are wrong, brother. What you feel now is fear. But you must not let it take you. Be strong. Listen to your own advice."

"Today was a disaster. Abby, I have no idea what we are looking for or why. I was just spouting off a bunch of thoughts, but the truth is I just don't know."

"But you said we should look here. Let's at least do that. You said we could check the stables and maybe some other places," she said. "You can't give up. Hannah...no, *all* of us, even Thomas, we are counting on you."

"I don't know, Abby. Being back here hasn't been what I thought it would be. I feel—I feel confused like I don't know what I'm doing."

"Looks to me like you have these bad guys pretty nervous. So you must be doing something right. Anyway, who would you call? Who else could help, but you? You're the one to help Hannah. God sent *you*." Abigail walked to the hitching post and gave her new gelding a pat. "You will do your job. Of that I have no doubt. But that is not what you are most afraid of, is it? You know, brother, you should speak your heart before it's too late."

"What are you talking about?" Elijah swallowed hard. "Facing up to *Dat,* you mean?"

"No. That's not what I mean, you daft man." Abigail frowned and lifted an eyebrow at him. Then she gave a nod back toward the house. "You wish it were you in there with Hannah in place of Thomas."

"Oh, please, Abby, she's got a killer after her and I'm doing a lousy job of keeping her alive. That's all that is between us right now. Hannah rejected me years ago. I have no interest in going through that again."

"What makes you so sure she'd reject you this time?" Abigail said. "Hannah and Peter were happy. She was a good wife to him. But it was you she loved enough to set free."

"Enough of this. You're making my head hurt worse than it already does." He turned away. "Let's go check the stables for this journal. Then I'll call McClendon and he can stay with the two of you tonight. I've got to go back before I…"

"Before you what, Elijah?" Abigail crossed her arms over her chest.

He looked up at the house, then back to his sister. "Before I do or say something that will hurt everyone."

FIFTEEN

Hannah's spirits lifted when Abigail invited her to spend the night at her home near Strasbourg. She couldn't remember the last time she'd slept away from Nolt Cottage—a night away from the constant reminders of Jessica and Peter, from her life before, would be a welcome reprieve.

After dinner, she packed one dress and climbed into Abigail's new carriage, while Abigail thanked Thomas for the gift of the horse and buggy. But when Elijah climbed in and sat beside her, a whole other feeling infused her blood.

"I thought you were going into the city to help with the search for Jackson, brother?" Abigail asked, sparing Hannah the need to frame the question as to why he was joining them.

Elijah flinched. "My partner, Tucci, has that under control. And…"

Hannah's heart froze at his pause.

"And what?" Abigail prodded.

"Well, tomorrow is my last day. *Dat,* he gave me three days. I'm going to use them. Hannah has decided to spend the night with you. So, if my first priority is to protect her, then you'd better make space for two guests."

"I knew you weren't a quitter." Abigail gave her new gelding a tap with the reins and they were off.

"Elijah, how would you feel about 'tending service with us in the morning?" Abigail asked.

Hannah had nearly forgotten that tomorrow was the Sabbath. A good word from Preacher Miller would do her well.

"I was welcomed at the gathering...but Sunday church? I don't think so."

"It is Providence that has brought you here, brother." Abigail smiled. "And it would please me very much. Mother, as well."

"And what do you think of my coming to Sunday church, Hannah?"

"Me? Well, I—I cannot say." Suddenly the image of Elijah in Plain dark trousers, a blue button-up shirt and black felt hat fell into her head. She hoped she did not blush. Why would she think such a silly thing? "I have no objections. But I cannot speak for others."

"Then you would welcome my coming?"

"Aye, I would."

Hannah was glad to see Abigail's home just in front of them and to have the end of this conversation.

It had been years since she'd been to see Abigail; Elijah's sister was a bit of an oddity in the *Ordnung,* not marrying, and living alone. Her place was large and fine. For years, she had been consulted for her knowledge as a *Doula* and as a doctors' aide at the hospital. Often, women would seek her help with womanly pains or other ailments when they did not need the consultation of a medical doctor.

Because of her clinic space, the house was more modern than most Amish. She even had more than one bathroom.

"One for clients. One for me," she explained.

And a fancy climate controller, which maintained seventy-two degrees even in summer.

"I can't have it too hot," she explained. "Breeds germs. I only use it in summer and it's still run by my oil tank."

It was late by the time they arrived, and after nearly no rest the night before, they were all ready to get to sleep.

Elijah insisted on sleeping downstairs on the couch, so Abigail showed Hannah to the spare bedroom, then brought her a clean towel and an extra blanket. Then she took a seat on the bed and smiled.

"You still love him, don't you?"

Heat rushed to Hannah's face. "Who do you speak of? Peter?"

"No. Of course you loved Peter, but he's gone with God now. I mean Elijah. You still love him. I can see it when you are together. You love him. Just as much as you did when you were young."

Hannah pressed her lips together and did not speak. To deny her statement would be a lie. To admit to it could be troublesome and unwise.

Abigail waited a moment. Then she stood and walked near to her. "You don't have to answer, Hannah. I see it in your face. What I really want to know is what you plan to do about it."

"To do?" Hannah tried to hide her face. She pretended to wipe it with the towel. "There is nothing to do. Your brother is part of a world that I care not to join. And today I saw what good he does." She dropped the towel and looked at her friend. "It is what he always wanted... I will admit that he is a good man, bound to the church or not. But he will be gone in another day. And I will go home. Where I belong."

"You admit nothing, Hannah." She turned toward the door. "God is giving you a second chance to be happy. But you and my brother are too proud to see it."

"Too proud?" Hannah stepped after her. "How

am I proud by choosing the Plain life? It's Elijah who…"

"It's Elijah who what?" Abigail asked.

"He will never forgive me for choosing Peter."

Abigail came back to stand next to her. She took one of her hands in her own. "Why did you choose Peter?"

"I loved him."

"You loved my brother. There was a reason. Was it for Jessica? To be her mother? I often wondered that you and Peter were never with child."

Hannah closed her eyes. She felt the tears coming. *Your brother wanted a family. He wanted to be a police officer. I could not give him those things.* Hannah wanted to say it, but she could not. She could not open her heart again. "It does not matter the reason. I hurt your brother and damaged what there was between us. What you see now is the pain I put there. Not love."

"Love can heal any hurt. Talk to him," Abigail said. "He has never loved another girl, Hannah. Only you."

Abigail left the room, but her words stayed and pressed on Hannah's heart. Exhausted and drained in every way, she lay on the bed and wept.

Elijah tossed and turned on Abigail's couch, unable to fall asleep despite his exhaustion. His aching skull was partly to blame, but it was more his racing mind that kept him awake—his thoughts jumping between the strange complications of Jessica's death, his mixed-up feelings about coming home and his even more complicated relationship with Hannah.

It wasn't just how he felt about her. He knew he loved her. He'd always loved her. She'd chosen someone else and he still loved her. None of that had changed. He had gone his own way and he knew he had been an instrument of God working as a police officer. So why did he feel called to come home now?

Was it for Hannah? Was it because he sought his father's approval so desperately?

It was both of those things and yet it somehow seemed like more than that. He half laughed to himself. His *Mamm* would have said it was further proof of his contrary nature, that he had dreaded coming home again, but now that he was there he wasn't sure he wanted to leave.

He missed the simple life. He missed his family. He missed that easy connection to his Father above. It was as if in coming home he'd come to a deeper understanding and need for all that he had once walked away from.

But how? How could he come back? His father did not accept him. Hannah would marry Thomas come November. That he could not bear to see. And God had called him to do police work.

He tossed again over the hard couch. Why did he feel so conflicted? God did not make mistakes. Elijah shook away the thoughts. He needed sleep and a clear head if he were going to figure this case out. There was still so much to work out and tomorrow, per his *Dat*'s decree, was his final day. He feared it would not be enough time and that he'd say goodbye to Hannah without giving her the peace of mind she so desperately needed.

A shadow fell over the room. Elijah welcomed the cloud. It would be much easier to sleep without so much moonlight, glaring in through the large windows.

He rolled onto his side and started to close his eyes. The shadow flickered. It grew larger. It went to the right. Then to the left.

That is no cloud. Someone is on the porch.

Without making a sound, Elijah slipped from the couch and moved away from the couch and window. The shadow formed once again on the wall across from him. Yep. He'd been right. That was not a cloud. It was a person, peering into the window—another uninvited guest, he thought, remembering the last two evenings.

Well, this time, Elijah was going to do the surprising and not the other way around. He slid away from the living room and moved quietly toward the back door of his sister's house.

SIXTEEN

Hannah awoke with a start. Heart racing, she sat upright in the bed, soaked in a sticky sweat. She'd fallen asleep over the bedsheets, fully dressed. Her cheeks were moist from half-dried tears. Her arms asleep from resting at strange angles. She scooted to the edge of the bed, trying to orient herself to the strange surroundings.

Abigail Miller's house. The shelves over the desk were heavy with books on homeopathic medicine and midwife practices. For the last five years, Abigail had helped to deliver the babies of almost every young Amish wife in Willow Trace and the surrounding towns. All of the young married women except for her. And that was the very reason she had been crying. Jessica was the only child she'd ever had—and now not only was Jessica gone, but the memory of her had been tainted by all the dreadful things Hannah had seen.

Hannah walked to the bathroom and washed her face. How had she gotten to be in this nightmare? It was all so confusing, so frightening, so... she didn't know what. She didn't know what to feel or how to feel it. She didn't know what to believe anymore. She thought of Abigail's encouraging her to talk to Elijah about her feelings. But hadn't she tried that last night in the buggy on the way back from the gathering? He had not responded. In fact, he had changed the subject and even seemed angry with her.

Not that any of it mattered. He was leaving. Tomorrow.

Hannah sighed away the sad thought, only to have it replaced with the other confusion in her head—that of this business with Jessica. Despite all the horrors she had seen that day, she could not bring herself to believe that Jessica would steal and lie and bring such shame to herself and all that she had professed to believe. It could not be possible. There had to be another reason Jessica was connected to all of this. Something that they were missing.

In her mind, she passed over her conversations with Brittney and Daniel. She suspected that both kids had lied at some point in their story. They were afraid, and rightfully so. But surely some of what they had told was truth. How did it all piece together?

Hannah couldn't help worrying about them both. Watching Brittney be dragged away had been terrifying. Neither she nor her father had been found.

At least, Elijah had "put a car on" Daniel, as he had phrased it, meaning he had police friends keeping an eye on the boy. Elijah had explained that not only would they keep him safe, but following Daniel might also lead them to the people tied to Jessica's murder.

How she both hoped for and feared the truth about her daughter. So many horrible things had been said about her. She had been to such a terrible place. Been so secretive and almost cruel to Daniel.

Only one thing gave Hannah a glimmer of hope, and that was Brittney. Brittney, who had been so worried that she would get Jessica in trouble. She'd sounded cognizant of the Amish ways. And she had stopped her stepfather when the man had had a gun to Hannah's head. Traded places with her. Maybe Brittney was not so bad as Daniel had made her sound.

Hannah also remembered a few other things that Daniel had said. First, that Jessica had carried a large bag with her. What large things would she be carrying? None of her clothing was missing. He'd also recounted that when he stopped her at the apartments, Jessica had claimed she was doing something good. For him to go home and that she would explain it later.

If Jessica were going to explain it later to Daniel, then she wasn't planning to run away. But doing something good? It was hard to believe there was any good to be done in that horrible place...unless...

Hannah straightened herself and headed out to wake Elijah. Finally she had an idea about Jessica that made sense to her. She hadn't figured all of the pieces out, but this part, this part about Jessica, this she felt certain of. She had to tell Elijah as soon as possible.

Passing through the small hallway into the living room, she found that the couch was empty. Hannah walked through the kitchen and then passed by the clinic.

"Elijah?"

There was no answer. Hannah shuddered. There was no chance Elijah had left them alone. Not after getting so cross with Thomas for having done that very thing.

Hannah turned back toward the bedrooms. She would wake Abigail. But something in the window caught her eye before she reached the hallway.

Hannah froze as fear prickled through her limbs. Had Jackson found them? She could still feel his massive fingers yanking at her head. Had he already gotten to Elijah? Hannah didn't know whether to run or scream or both.

She watched as the dark figure melted back into the night without a sound. Then she sprinted back to Abigail's room. She wasn't going to sit there like an easy target. Not tonight. Not again.

"Abigail, wake up. Elijah is gone and I saw someone looking in the windows."

"What?" Abigail sat up. "Hannah? Are you okay?"

"Wake up. Something is happening." Hannah repeated the situation. "I think they found us."

Abigail looked pensive for a second. Then she got up and headed to her own window to peer out. "Yes. Could be so," she said. "Or it could be a patient?"

"But where is your brother? He wouldn't have left us without saying so."

"Probably so. We should call the police."

"You have a phone?"

"Only for work. I have to know when a patient is going into labor, you know." Abigail headed for the hallway. "Come. It's in the kitchen."

A light knock sounded at the door.

Abigail and Hannah looked at each other. Hannah could feel her heart pounding in her chest. But Abigail relaxed some and headed to the door.

"What are you doing?"

"Intruders don't knock." Abigail turned to the door and called out. "Who is it?"

"Please, let me in. Hurry. Please." The voice was weak and soft like that of a child.

Abigail looked back one more time at Hannah and then headed on to the door. Heaven help them if this were a trick. But they could hardly ignore the desperation in the voice behind the door. Still, where was Elijah? She wished Elijah were there.

"Do I know you?" Abigail asked with a shrug.

"It's Brittney. Brittney Baker. I know it's late. I'm sorry. I didn't know where else to go. You said I could come. Please let me in."

Abigail unlocked the front door. Hannah hit the light switch. Brittney hobbled into the house. She was cut, bruised, bleeding.

Elijah came up behind the porch behind her. He was putting his gun away. "I nearly took you out, young lady. You shouldn't go around peeking into the windows like you did. Next time try the front door first."

"I am sorry. I—I—"

Elijah caught her before she hit the floor. "Good gracious. She's been beaten nearly to death."

"Quick. Take her to the clinic," Abigail told him.

Elijah picked the girl up and carried her to Abigail's examination room.

Her eyes fluttered as Elijah placed her on the table.

"Dear child, what has happened to you?" Hannah asked.

"I just don't know where it is." She tried to lift herself up.

"Shh. Don't try to talk. Just rest." Hannah turned to Abigail. "What can I do to help?"

"Keep her quiet. And still." Abigail busied herself preparing bandages and solutions. "We'll have to cut off those clothes and dress all those wounds. She may need blood."

"Can you tend to her, Abby? Without paramedics?" Elijah asked.

"I can try. I think Jackson did this to her," Abigail said. They checked her limbs, face and neck for more bruising and other injuries.

"I know Jackson did it." Elijah pointed to a cut on the girl's face. "See? Here is a mark from the ring he wears on his right hand." He put a hand to the girl's forehead and she opened her eyes. "Do you know where he is?"

She was too weak to answer.

"You can interrogate later." Abigail shooed him from the clinic space.

Hannah was filled with anger thinking of the horrible man who'd put this girl in such a state. It made her sick and enraged all at once. And there was so much blood. She couldn't help thinking of Jessica.

But for the next few hours, she and Abigail tended to the poor beaten girl. She was in and out of consciousness. Mercifully, nothing was broken, but she was still suffering from a severe concussion and bruising such as Hannah had never seen. And it all confirmed the idea she'd had earlier about her stepdaughter.

When they'd finished, they dressed her in some of Abigail's clothing, moved her to the couch and Abigail began pouring tea down her throat.

"Drink up. It will help with the swelling and the pain."

"It's a wonder you made it all the way out to Lancaster without passing out," Elijah said. "Where is Jackson? Where did he take you?"

"What is this?" She choked at the taste of the tea.

"Lotus." Abigail smiled with pride, then looked at her brother. "You have to report this."

"No. No." Brittney coughed out the words. "No report. I thought that was the Amish way. No outside help. That's why I came here."

"Well, yes, but you aren't Amish," Abigail said. "And this isn't something we can ignore. He could kill you."

"He won't kill me," she said. "He always knows when to stop. You are wasting your time if you report this. Actually, it will just make things worse. I'll have to go back to him. They'll call him. They always call him. What I really want is to stay here. Please promise me you won't call."

"We can't promise that, Brittney," Elijah said.

"I am a police officer. You are underage and have to be either in the care of your legal guardian or Social Services. I can hold off for a bit, but eventually I have to report a case of child abuse. At least that will get you out of his custody."

"But don't you see? He is the police, too." She shook her head. "You make a report. He makes it disappear. You say Flynn Jackson. He makes the report says Christopher Jones, or George Smith. He has the system in his pocket."

"He doesn't have *me* in his pocket," Elijah said.

"Jessica was trying to get you out of there, wasn't she?" Hannah asked.

"Yes. She was. I saw Jessica at a party. She looked so perfect. So peaceful. So happy. I knew she had something that I didn't. And I wanted it. So I asked her. I asked her about your God. And when I heard of His love and acceptance, I knew I belonged to Him. I just didn't know how to get away from Flynn."

"But Jessica had a plan?" Elijah asked.

The girl nodded. "She said I could come here. Because of the Amish way. No help from the authorities. She said that Flynn wouldn't be able to find me here."

"She was trying to help this poor girl," Abigail repeated proudly. She patted Hannah's hand. "See? You were a great mother. Jessica was a sweet girl. She was trying to help."

Hannah fought tears.

"Now I'm off to fix everyone some tea." Abigail hurried off to the kitchen.

Hannah took a step toward the girl. "So all this is due to Jessica trying to help you?" Brittney nodded, and the tears slid down Hannah's soft cheeks.

He walked over and touched Hannah's shoulder. "Your daughter made a difference. I know it doesn't bring her back. But knowing must give you some peace. She made a difference. *You* made a difference. This girl will never be the same."

She looked up and smiled at him. "It does not take my sadness. But, yes, it gives me peace."

Abigail bustled back into the room with a tray of steaming teas.

"I don't think you can get her to drink anymore." Elijah pointed out that Brittney had dozed off.

"This is for you." Abigail handed a cup of tea to both Hannah and him.

"For us?" they said together.

"Yes, it's passion flower."

Passion flower? Hannah could already feel the blush on her cheeks. Why was Abigail pushing this so hard? Didn't she see that it wasn't meant to be?

"It's for sleeping," Abigail said with a teasing tone. "You both need to rest."

* * *

Although still stiff and bruised, Brittney was much recovered by morning. The ladies tended to her with a full breakfast and much fussing.

Elijah sat at the other end of the table with his cup of black coffee and slice of buttered toast, alternating thoughts between the case and how today was his last day in Willow Trace.

"You look much better, Brittney."

"Thanks. Thanks to all of you," she said. "And especially for not calling the cops. You don't understand—"

"We do," Elijah said. "We do understand. And we want to help, but you have to talk to us so that we can stop Jackson once and for all. Did he kill Jessica?"

Her eyes went wide. "I don't think so."

"But he was with her that night?"

She nodded hesitantly. "Yes."

Elijah leaned forward with his cup of coffee. "Who else was there? Why didn't you tell us any of this when we were there?"

"I couldn't talk in the apartment, you know." Brittney pushed a loose lock of hair out of her eyes. "You never know who's listening. That's what happened with Jessica."

"*What* happened with Jessica?" Elijah pressed her.

"Well, I don't know all of it." Brittney pressed

her lips together and took a long sip of her tea. "She came over and we were going to leave. Leave Flynn. She said I could come here and he'd never find me. But…"

"It's okay," Hannah encouraged her. "Keep going. We want to know."

"Well, it was all going great, until Jackson showed up."

"*What* happened with Jackson?" Elijah was impatient for answers. It wasn't that he didn't trust that Brittney wanted a different life and now knew God's love. He just didn't trust that she was telling the hundred percent truth. She was scared. And used to a world where steering people the wrong way to protect yourself was a way of life. But lies were often mixed with some truth, and if she told the right things, if he asked the right questions, he could put it all together and maybe figure out where Jackson was. Today. His last day.

"Well, like I said, she came to the apartment. But we didn't get out in time."

"Who found you?"

"Flynn and Mr. Krups," she said as if they should have already known.

"Mr. Krups?"

"Yeah. That's who wants the journal. Mr. Krups. Why else do you think Flynn is so crazy? If he doesn't get that journal back, Mr. Krups will…well, *he* won't do it…but let's just say it won't be too good for Flynn."

"Wait a minute. Wait a minute." Elijah shook his head. "Your dad works for Norton Krups? I thought he worked for Philadelphia Party Rentals?"

"Stepdad," she corrected him quickly. "The party rental place is a front. I thought everyone in Philly knew that."

"So, it's Norton Krups's journal that everyone is looking for? How or why did Jessica get a hold of something like that? Or *did* she actually get a hold of it?"

Brittney looked around the room at each of them. Her eyes almost popped out of her head. "Man, you guys really don't know anything, do you?"

"Apparently not." Elijah ran his hands through his hair. How could he take down someone as connected and powerful as Norton Krups?

"And it's not really a journal, either," she added. "It's an electronic device that holds security codes. And not just for Krups. I heard Flynn bragging to someone that the journal had all the codes connected with Dutch Confidential security systems and that he could steal information without being detected. Can you imagine? Even government systems use that company."

"I do not understand. Who is this Krups?" Hannah asked.

Elijah paused. How did you describe a guy like Krups to a lady like Hannah? "He's a respected businessman who has been suspected of illegal activities, gunrunning, drugs, murder. But no one has ever been able to prove it." Elijah turned back to Brittney. "So, why did Jessica take this journal? What was she planning to do with these codes?"

"Actually, I took the journal." She dropped her head. "One day, I was so mad at Flynn. He kept bragging about how great it was and how Krups was going to make him top dog. Then as usual, he got drunk and hit me for leaving a dish out or something. Anyway, I took it and I asked Jessica to hide it."

"And she agreed to this?" Hannah asked.

"Yes. I told her what it was and what Flynn and Krups could do with it and so she thought it was good that they not have it anymore. *A good thing to do,* she said." Brittney smiled.

Elijah couldn't help grinning. He turned to Hannah and explained. "If what Brittney says is true, you can be sure that Krups and Jackson were going to use these codes to do something illegal. Jessica thought that it was a good thing to stop them."

"Right," Brittney said. "And she also figured that Flynn would be so freaked out about losing the journal that he wouldn't notice me leaving. She said once I turned eighteen I could hand it over to the authorities and get Flynn in lots of trouble."

"So, where did Jessica put the device?"

"That I don't know. Jessica thought it would be better if she didn't tell me. And then if Flynn asked me about it, I wouldn't have to lie."

"What happened the day Jessica came to see you?" Hannah asked.

"We were going to come here. It's only a few weeks until my birthday. Then I would be eighteen." A sad expression covered her face. Her eyes teared and she stared at the floor, speaking slowly. "Jessica thought her mom would let me stay for a bit. She said as long as I did my work and went to church, I'd be *Welkommen*."

"So, what happened?"

"We didn't make it. Flynn showed up. Krups showed up. Somehow Flynn realized that I took the journal. I don't know how he figured it out, but he did. I was so scared. But Jessica was brave. She talked right back to Flynn and Mr. Krups. Told them they could have the codes back as soon as Flynn signed over my guardianship."

Elijah shook his head. "Jessica was brave. Too brave."

"What do you mean?" Hannah asked.

"Well, a man like Krups isn't going to…" Elijah

paused. "He isn't going to negotiate with a couple of teenagers."

"So he killed her." Hannah sighed.

Brittney looked down. "I don't know. They separated us. Flynn took me inside the apartment. Krups grabbed Jessica…that was the last time I saw her."

Elijah rubbed his face with his hands. Krups. Jackson worked for Krups. Everyone worked for Krups. And Jessica had died at their hands keeping this secret in hopes of saving a poor girl from a home where no one wanted her. Hannah had been right all along. She'd raised a noble and brave daughter. Her actions reminded him of how he'd felt when he first had joined the force—he'd thought stopping a criminal would be as easy as finding them.

Hannah stood, wringing her hands in her apron. "Okay. Now I understand why they searched our house and our stable, but why me? Why do they think I know where this journal is? I know nothing."

Brittney shrugged and started to cry again.

Eli frowned. The girl knew why Hannah was a target. But still there was something she wasn't saying. He wondered how detrimental her silence would be.

"Well, I'd say that's enough questions for now." Abigail walked over to where Brittney sat. She knelt down beside her and spoke. "I am very glad you have come, Brittney. And we thank you for the truth. You know it is okay to be sad." She glanced at Hannah as she spoke. "But wasn't it good to have someone in the world to love you? Even if it is just for a short time. Treasure your friendship with Jessica. It was from God, who loves you. That is the Amish way. We don't understand why she had to leave us so soon, but we are ever thankful that we had her here with us for the time that we did. Same as her *Dat.* He would have been proud of her."

Abigail rose again and helped the girl up from the couch. "Come now. Time for another lotus tea."

She led Brittney away to the kitchen.

Elijah agreed that she needed a break even though he had more questions. He wasn't even sure the girl could answer his questions.

What they really needed was to find Jackson. And maybe, with the help of God, find the journal of codes. If they could do that, they could possibly take Krups down, too. There was still so much uncertainty, so many things they didn't know. Well, at least, Hannah had one account of Jessica that was favorable. No one could be pleased with the outcome, but it seemed the girl's heart had been in the right place.

He turned to Hannah. He caught the curves of

her profile as she looked away from him. He admired the fullness of her lips and long dark lashes that blinked away the abundance of moisture in her eyes. How beautiful she was. How he longed to comfort her in her moment of suffering. He watched a moment as she continued to play nervously with the white cloth of her apron.

"Jessica died trying to help this girl." Elijah turned away as he spoke, for fear she'd see the love in his eyes. "She was brave and bold. I'm sorry I didn't know her better."

"Aye, but she was a *gut* girl." Hannah was trying to control her voice and yet it faltered with emotion.

Elijah glanced to the kitchen, where Brittney had gone. "I think we should finish what she started. We should help this girl."

Hannah rose from her chair and moved toward him. She grasped his hands and looked deep into his eyes. "Always, I knew Jessica was a *gut* girl. She had a heart only to help others. Like you, Elijah. God has brought you here to make this right."

Elijah released her hands, placed his gently against her cheeks and wiped her tears with his thumbs. Closing her eyes, she leaned into his palms, welcoming his touch. Her hands lifted up and rested on his shoulders. His pulse raced as he lowered his head toward her soft lips.

The beep of his cell phone sounded. He wanted

to ignore it. He wanted to kiss her. Instead, he stepped back and pulled his phone from his pocket.

"Miller here," he answered.

"We got Jackson," Tucci said. "But you've got to get here fast. I won't be able to hold him long."

"What is it?" Hannah asked when he pocketed his phone and turned away.

"They got him. They got Jackson. I have to go."

Without a kiss.

SEVENTEEN

Hannah had thought this would feel different. She had thought that finding out about Jessica would give her some closure. But instead it seemed as though there were only more questions. Where was this journal? And why did anyone think she had it?

Not that it mattered anymore. Elijah had Jackson. Jackson would give them this Krups person and the whole thing would be over.

Which meant not getting to see Elijah anymore. She definitely felt confused about that. And there she had just nearly let him kiss her. What was she thinking? Good thing his phone had rung. And now he was gone.

"Where is Brittney?" Hannah asked as she and Abigail dried the morning dishes.

"She's gone to rest." Abigail eyed her with suspicion. "What's on your mind? I know when a woman wants to talk."

Hannah shrugged. "What's not on my mind—

the journal, this poor child's father, what I'm going to do when this—"

"Your feelings for my brother..." Abigail added.

Hannah took another plate and began to dry. Yes, that was on her mind but it shouldn't be.

"I know I shouldn't pry, but you both are so worried the other doesn't want to hear what you have to say that..." Abigail took the drying towel from Hannah's hands and steered her toward a chair at the kitchen table. "I saw you holding his hand. Did you talk about your feelings? About the future?"

"I told you, Abigail, it's not meant to be."

"How do you know what God's plan is? You don't."

"No. I don't. But I know I'll be shunned if I take on seriously with your brother. And I'll hurt Thomas, which I would never want to do. He's been very kind."

"Thomas is your brother. And he loves you. He isn't going to be surprised by this. If he is protective, it's because he doesn't want you to get hurt. And that's only because he doesn't know my brother. But I do and I know Elijah loves you."

Hannah shook her head. "Sometimes love isn't enough. Sometimes people need different things. You know I don't regret the decision I made. I was a good wife to Peter and I cared for him. I missed Elijah's friendship, but I knew he was happy being a cop and I was so happy to be a mother to Jessica." She sat down and sighed.

"But what about now?" Abigail smiled and took the seat opposite her.

Hannah smiled and nodded. "I don't think your brother wants to come back here."

"You are wrong about that. I saw him yesterday. Coming back is exactly what Elijah wants. He wants family. He told me so himself."

Exactly. And I cannot give him one. "I don't know. I tried to talk with him last night. He did not seem interested in hearing my feelings."

"*Ack.* He is only afraid. That is why I push you. You are brave, Hannah. Just like Jessica."

"Not anymore. Not after losing Peter and Jessica."

"You must be brave." Abigail patted her hand. "Be brave with your heart again."

"It's not my heart that I fear. It's that I cannot…" Hannah paused. *I cannot tell him that I cannot give him a family….*

"You cannot what? Will you not speak to him?"

Hannah shook her head. "There are things you do not know, Abigail. It is not as simple as you believe."

"I never said it would be simple." Abigail smiled. "I only said you should be honest. At least, think on it. I'm going to check on our patient. Then perhaps we could head to Sunday service."

Hannah stopped her. "What do you think will happen to the girl? Will she have to go back to her stepfather?"

"No. Elijah will not let that happen. She's almost eighteen, which means she'll soon be legally independent—but she will still need some guidance and a way to support herself." Abigail clasped her hands together at her chest. "Elijah is arranging for her to stay here until I make some arrangements for her. It's complicated, but I think she'll be okay."

"I'd like to help," Hannah said.

"Good. I'd like for you to help."

The exchange of words was like a pact between sisters and it warmed Hannah through. Maybe Abigail was right. Maybe everything would work out somehow. She started away to fetch her best dress for Sunday church. Service was at the Stottlemeyers', just a five-minute walk from Abigail's.

"Hannah?" Abigail walked back in from the hallway. "I was thinking if you can't talk to my brother and you don't want to stay on with the Nolts—"

"I never said I didn't want to—"

Abigail waved her hands in the air. "Hear me out. I was just thinking that it must be hard for you to stay on without Jessica there."

"*Jah.* It is."

"Well, you are welcome to stay here. As long as you need. I would welcome the company."

"That is most kind. But I couldn't pay you."

"You could work for me," she said. "I need someone to tend to the garden and the cleaning while I am seeing patients."

Hannah took in her words.

"Think that over, too," Abigail said, and turned away.

"I will," Hannah said. "Now let's off to church and some time to pray. You have my head spinning, Abigail. I need some time to listen to God and settle it again."

After the call from Tucci, Elijah knew two things. First, that his partner was sticking his neck out in a big way by bringing Jackson in under a false name for him.

Secondly, Elijah knew this was his best chance to help Hannah and Willow Trace. He had to ask the right questions. There was no time to make mistakes. If only he could focus, he could be sure to do that. But that wasn't so easy to do, when he couldn't stop thinking about that near kiss.

Get a grip, Miller. Strange vibes flowed through him as he entered the station. Something was different. He ignored the uncomfortable feelings and found his partner waiting for him in the hallway.

"I got him in interrogation five," Tucci said. "I haven't asked him a thing. He's just been sitting there for an hour. He's starting to sweat."

"Where did you find him?"

"At a coffee shop in Kennett Square," Tucci said. "A patrolman walked in and recognized his face from the bulletin yesterday."

"Great. Then all his friends will know he's here."

"Not much we can do about that," Tucci replied. "But he was stupid and sloppy yesterday. Too many people saw him. He assaulted you. Held a woman at gunpoint—"

"Beat his teenaged stepdaughter to near death," Elijah added. "She showed up at my sister's in the middle of the night. Abigail took pictures."

"Rape?"

He shook his head. "My sister is a midwife and nursed her last night. She says no signs of rape. But the girl told us a lot this morning."

Elijah filled Tucci in while pouring himself a tall cup of coffee, and headed into the room with Jackson.

"Good morning, Flynn. So good of you to come visit me and see how I'm doing. I really appreciate that because I have some questions for you."

Jackson barely lifted his eyes. "I don't know you. So I don't know what you're talking about."

Elijah spotted the large ring that had marred

Brittney's face. "Tucci, I need someone to bag and analyze this ring, please."

"Don't you need a warrant for those?" Jackson said. "I want my lawyer."

"We're trying to get your lawyer, Flynn. But he's not answering his phone. And no, I don't need a warrant. I don't even need the ring or the boot." He pulled out his cell phone and showed Jackson a picture of Brittney's bruised face and then a picture of the cut on his head. "Between these pictures and many eyewitnesses, I think you'd better hand it over. The best thing you can do is confess. Even your lawyer would tell you that. Plead guilty and maybe the courts will have some mercy. What do you say, Jackson?"

"Confess to what?" Jackson laughed. "You got nothing. In about thirty minutes I'll be walking out of here."

"Well, then why don't we chat for those thirty minutes?"

"I don't have anything to say to you."

"What if I told you I found that journal of codes that you've been looking for? Have anything to say then? If I hand that over to someone—like, let's say, Norton Krups—then maybe you won't be walking in thirty minutes."

"You don't have that journal." He sneered. "You're bluffing."

"How does Mr. Krups feel about you getting

duped by a couple of teenaged girls, huh?" Elijah taunted him. He had a feeling that Jackson was the type to lose it if he got mad. And if he lost it, he might say something useful. "So that was probably a career buster for you. Even though you're the one who stole the codes from Dutch Confidential, you also lost them before getting them to Krups. Sort of knocked you down the crime ladder a good ways."

Jackson shifted uncomfortably in his chair. Elijah continued with the humiliation tactic.

"I'll bet Mr. Krups had some big plans for all those codes. But you blew it. Let a couple of little girls steal it right out from under your nose."

"What do you want, Detective Miller?" Jackson crossed his hands over his chest. "You want me to help you get Krups? I'm dead if I do that."

"You're dead if you don't do it."

"What are you talking about?"

"I'm talking about you murdering an Amish teenaged girl. I'm talking maximum security for an ex-cop. The guards will hate you. The inmates will hate you. It will be a long, long life sentence."

Jackson stood, throwing his hands in the air in protest. His anger now was turning to fear. "Murder? I didn't murder anyone. I trade information and do favors for people. I don't kill."

"Jessica Nolt. She was last seen with you before she was found with a slit neck. We have pictures of what you did to your own stepdaughter. We saw you with a knife under her chin. I doubt a jury will think it much of a stretch to believe you used that knife on another child." Elijah stood and walked to the door. "You should have stuck to being a dirty cop. Murder is a deadly business."

"Wait," Jackson said before Elijah had stepped out of the room. "Just...just wait. Let's talk."

EIGHTEEN

Hannah and Abigail dressed and helped Brittney into an old dress of Abigail's since her own clothes had been so badly stained and cut.

"It's a little long." Hannah giggled. Abigail was a good three inches taller than the teen. "But it will do."

"It's a little stiff and itchy," Brittney said.

"*Jah.* Just be thankful you don't have to pin it together like some of the Amish," Hannah said.

"Pin it?" Brittney scrunched up her nose.

"*Jah,* many Amish think hooks and eyes are too fancy," Abigail said. "They use straight pins to fasten the skirt and apron together."

Brittney seemed to consider that for a moment. "Don't they stick into you when you move?"

"*Nein.* Not if you pin it correctly."

Brittney giggled. "Jessica told me how different it is here. She said that you try not to be noticed here. And there *we* are, back in the city, squeez-

ing into the tightest jeans possible, hoping someone will look."

"We look upward," Abigail said. "To the Lord."

"I want to learn how to do that, too." A worried
expression covered Brittney's face.

"You know they won't be able to keep Flynn,"
she said. "He gets questioned all the time, but
never charged with anything. And if he did, then
where would I go?"

Hannah looked to Abigail and back to Brittney.
"I do not understand the English system, Brittney.
But I have faith in God and in Elijah that you will
not be harmed again. If I have to stand between
you and that horrible man to prevent it, I will. Just
like Jessica. I give you my promise."

"And now we are off to church?" Hannah asked
Abigail, wondering if the girl was too frail to
walk the short distance to the Stottlemeyers' for
church.

"How would you like that, Brittney?" Abigail
said. "It's not far today. Just around the corner.
If you get tired, we can find you a comfortable
spot there to rest. Or we can return."

The girl's expression perked up a bit. "I suppose I'm already dressed for it. Let's go."

"Gut." Hannah was pleased. "Daniel and Jessica's other friends will be there. You can socialize
with them after the service, if you feel up to it."

"Daniel?" Brittney looked worried again. "I'm sure he won't be glad to see me."

Hannah patted her shoulder. "That is not true. You have much to learn about the Amish. We are very forgiving."

"Have you talked to him about Jessica and the journal?" Brittney asked.

"*Jah,* he was looking for it in our house the other night." Hannah said. "Why?"

Brittney paused before speaking, as if she weren't sure how she wanted to answer. "Just wondering if he had talked to you about stuff. That's all."

Hannah could see behind Brittney's brown eyes that *that wasn't all*. There was something else the girl knew and it had something to do with Daniel.

The day was warm and after the service Hannah helped the other women set tables on the front lawn for the midday meal.

Abigail had taken Brittney to the back porch to rest for a bit. Hannah could only imagine that listening to a two-hour sermon in a language one didn't understand would be fatiguing for even someone in the best of health. After all that Brittney had been through, she had to have been exhausted. Hannah figured that as soon as she'd helped set up the meal, she and Abigail could help

Brittney back to Abigail's so that the girl could get some proper rest.

Before leaving, Hannah had also thought to speak to Daniel. She had seen him earlier sitting with his family. He had looked more than surprised when he saw Brittney sitting with herself and Abigail. Earlier at the house, Brittney's comment about Daniel had her thinking that maybe he knew more than he had told them. As Elijah had said to her, *sometimes we know things that we don't think are important to a case, but they are.* He had explained that part of his job was to get all of that information from witnesses and victims and other parties and put it together, until it made sense.

She wished Elijah were there now so that she would know what questions to ask Daniel. She wasn't sure at all how to start a conversation with him about the journal and what he knew about it.

Truth was, she wished Elijah were there anyway. During the service, she had thought and prayed heavily about the things Abigail had mentioned. She wanted to talk to Elijah about her feelings, but she didn't know if she could be that brave. And in the end, what would it matter? Elijah would go back to the city and his work and she would stay in Willow Trace.

Hannah carried out the drinks and saw that most of the work had been done. She would look for Daniel. Glancing across the lawn, she saw him crossing the grassy paddock in front of the stable. He glanced her way. Hannah put down the two pitchers of tea she carried and tried to motion him over, but he turned away and slipped quickly behind the Stottlemeyers' barn. There wasn't anything she knew of behind that barn. Curious, she decided to follow after him.

She was halfway across the lawn when she realized she should tell Abigail her plan. It would take but a second to walk by the back porch. Abigail sat upright in a white wooden rocker and was sleeping like a baby. Hannah would have laughed aloud except that as she got closer she noticed the long swing next to Abigail—the swing on which Brittney had been resting—was empty.

Brittney was missing.

"I didn't murder anybody. You got the wrong guy for that." Jackson shook his head back and forth.

Elijah turned and glared hard at him. The brutish man ran his thick hands through short red hair.

"Then who did? You were with her. You dumped her at the barn. Your black sedan was seen leaving the site. I'm thinking we'll find trace evidence once the car is examined."

Jackson grumbled, "She's my daughter's friend. I gave her a ride."

"You don't think we'll find her blood? What about the other Amish kid, Daniel? He can identify you, too."

"But he can't say I killed her, because I didn't. I didn't touch that little girl. I swear. And if Brittney or that other punk kid says I did, then they're lying." The color of Jackson's cheeks now matched his hair. "Krups did it. He's crazy all of a sudden. He'll kill anybody to get those codes back. He thinks that afterward he can get into the right system and change the history on the computer."

"And that's why he doesn't kill you? Because he needs you to get the codes?" Elijah slammed the file folder down on the table and looked into the two-way mirror with a shrug. This discovery was not going to work in their favor. Jackson was mad enough to point the finger at Krups for the murder charge, but he wasn't scared because as long as those codes were still out there, Krups wouldn't hurt him.

"Okay, let's say I believe you for one second. Tell me why Krups killed the one person who knew where the codes were?"

"He didn't mean to kill her," Jackson said. "Don't get me wrong. He probably would have anyway, once he got the journal. But he didn't mean to when it happened."

"When what happened?"

"Krups was knocking her around, trying to get her to talk. He broke a bottle against the wall to scare her. But when he pushed her a little too hard, she fell. Krups reached out with the sharp glass in his hand. It went clean across her throat as she tripped down the stairs. Then he was just angry because he still didn't have the codes."

"If your story is true, that's still murder and you're an accessory." Elijah walked back and leaned his weight over table toward Jackson.

"I can't give you Krups," he said.

"Then tell me why you and Krups are after Daniel and Hannah. What makes you think they can lead you to the journal?"

"The girl said so." Jackson was very matter-of-fact. "Krups was scaring her and pushing her around and her last words were 'don't hurt my *Mamm* or Daniel.' They must know something. Otherwise, why would we hurt them?"

"A dying child calls out for her mother and friend and that's what you guys are going on? Are you kidding me?"

"I'm not. And Brittney confirmed her claim. She'd told my daughter nearly the same thing— that no one knew exactly where the codes were but that Daniel and her *Mamm* could find them if they had to. That's all we had. Brittney would have told us if she'd known anything else. Krups can be very persuasive."

"But, let me guess, you made her talk." Elijah felt his head begin to ache. "Just tell me where Krups is and we'll drop the accessory to murder charge."

"You're not a D.A. You can't negotiate that." Jackson shook his head. "Look, even if you have the journal, which I don't believe you do, you can't tie it to Krups. You can't get to him. It's impossible. He dots every *i* and crosses every *t*. You are wasting your time."

"Like getting you was impossible?" Elijah smiled. "Everyone has an Achilles' heel."

"Yeah, well, if he's got one it's that journal, which you don't have, or this conversation would be going in a completely different direction."

Elijah sighed in frustration. He'd hoped for more from Jackson, but he should have known he wouldn't get it.

A knock sounded at the interrogation room door. Tucci cracked the door slightly and popped his head in. "Phone call for you, Miller."

Elijah nodded. He stepped out of the small interrogation room, closed the door behind him and reached for the phone from his partner.

"Miller here," he answered.

Tucci hung close as if waiting to see his response.

"Elijah, we need your help." The voice on the

line was not any he'd expected—it was deep and tight and speaking the language of his youth. "We need your help, son."

"*Dat?* What it?" Elijah's pulse spiked.

"They're all missing—Hannah, Abigail, the *Englischer* girl, even Daniel. They were here at the Stottlemeyers' for Sunday church. And now they aren't. Thomas drove over to Abigail's place and they aren't there, either. We're quite afraid something has happened. The People are all together praying. Come, my son. Come and help us find them."

"Keep everyone praying. I'll be right there, *Dat*."

NINETEEN

"Hurry, Abigail," Hannah said. "There she goes, behind the stable, just like Daniel. We don't want to lose sight of her."

Hannah hurried toward the Stottlemeyers' stable, tugging Abigail behind her.

"Where in the world could she be going?" Abigail said. "She doesn't know her way around here."

"No, but Daniel does. She's following him. I saw him go around the stable first. Then I came to check on you, and Brittney had just left. I looked up across the lawn and spotted her exactly where I had seen Daniel."

"But what can they be about, running off from Sunday gathering into these woods?" Abigail asked.

"Actually, I think I know where they are going." Hannah shook her head. "And I cannot believe I did not think of this place before. It makes perfect sense now."

"What makes perfect sense?"

"The hiding place. Jessica's hiding place."

"You mean Brittney and Daniel are going after the journal? You think they know where Jessica hid it?"

"*Jah,* that is exactly what I think."

"Don't you think we'd get more information if we stayed and continued to question Jackson? He knew Krups was headed out there. He as much as said so. He probably set the whole thing up."

"I don't think so. We have to get started while the trail is still at least warm."

"But we couldn't find Jackson yesterday and he'd been right under our noses in the city with nowhere to go." Tucci glanced over at Elijah as they sped over the Pennsylvania countryside. "If Krups has Hannah and your sister, then how in the world do you think we're going to locate them in the boondocks of Lancaster County? He's had an hour start on us."

"You forget that I know those boondocks." Not to mention his *Dat* had asked him to come. His *Dat* actually called him and asked for his help as a cop and as his son. Elijah closed his eyes and tried to visualize what might have happened at the farm to Hannah, Abigail and Brittney. They'd gone to Sunday church. Listened to the preaching. Everyone would have seen them. Brittney

would have been introduced to the other teens—
Daniel included. Hannah would have helped with
the Sunday meal. He'd seen at his cousin John's
that Hannah sort of took charge in this activity. She would have been missed if she had not
been there helping. By the time his *Dat* had called
him at the station, the Sunday meal would have
normally started. Now everyone was gathered to
pray that they found Hannah, Abigail, Daniel and
the *Englischer* girl.

He too prayed.

"Are you sure you know the way?" Abigail
asked Hannah for the third time since they'd
started into the woods behind the Stottlemeyers'
barn. "We haven't seen either Brittney or Daniel
since we first came into the trees."

"Well, this isn't the usual way to get to Cy-
prus Cabin, but I know we're heading in the
right direction." Hannah climbed over a patch of
briars. "In fact, we should be getting very
close." She lowered her voice. "Did you know
the hunting lodge is over one hundred fifty years
old? This land used to belong to some wealthy
Englischer from the city before the Stottlemeyer
family bought it up. At one time, I think the cabin
must have been quite nice. Not much to it anymore. But when Jessica was very young, I took

her there and let her play 'house' while I worked on some knitting or whatnot."

"So you and Elijah had a secret love shack?" Abigail teased.

"*Ack*. No." Hannah blushed. "Your brother was a perfect gentleman...although he might have stolen a kiss or two. Shh. There it is."

Hannah directed Abigail to look through a small clearing so that she could see the dilapidated cabin ahead. As she had remembered, not much was left of it, no windows and doors. Just the clapboard siding and roof remained. Vines and trees had grown thick around it—its grays and greens still soft and inviting.

"It's charming." Abigail smiled.

"I hear voices," Hannah warned her.

The two women stalked closer to the small structure, trying to keep themselves hidden in the brush. Through the window holes, Hannah spotted Daniel and Brittney. They seemed to be in the midst of an argument.

"Come on," Hannah said to Abigail. "Let's see if they found the journal. I want to see this thing that has wreaked havoc on all our lives."

Elijah and Mitchell arrived in Lancaster from the city in record time and drove straight to Stottlemeyer's where much of the Sunday gathering had disbursed. A few families had gone home in order to be on the lookout for their missing friends. Only a few remained huddled in prayer and communion. Among the women, Elijah spotted his mother.

He gave her a strong, steady embrace.

"Your father's gone home in case of any news there." Her face was drawn with worry.

"What can you tell me? Where did you see them last?" Elijah asked her.

She shook her head and shrugged. "After service, Abigail and the *Englischer* girl were resting on the back porch. Hannah was directing Sunday meal as always. Then all of a sudden they were all gone. It was time to sit down and eat and we couldn't find any of them. Kasey and Geoffrey said that Daniel was gone, too. Your father sent Thomas to Abigail's to see if they had walked home, even though I can't imagine them doing that without speaking to a soul."

Elijah nodded. "Has anyone seen any strangers about today? Tourists? Passing cars? Vans? Anything unusual?"

The women shook their heads.

Elijah's hope was fading as he looked around at the vast countryside around them. "Did the women arrive in a buggy?"

"No, by foot."

"And Daniel?"

"Rode in with his family," his *mamm* answered. "They are still here and so is the buggy."

"Any of Stottlemeyer's horses missing?"

"Nary a one. Mr. Stottlemeyer went and counted them all."

"Are Kasey and Geoffrey still here?"

"*Jah,* just there." His mother pointed across the lawn.

He nodded for Tucci to follow him over to the group of teens. "Maybe Daniel said something to his friends?"

"I sure hope so. 'Cause otherwise, we got nothing. No vehicle to follow. No trail. Nothing to put out an APB on. They haven't been missing long enough to conduct a search."

"Well, under the circumstances, we can call in some local cars to troll the surrounding areas." Elijah shook his head. "I should have insisted that car stay on Daniel. Or that he stay with me."

"He had a detail?"

"Yes, but only for twenty-four hours. You know, budget cuts. Lack of officers on duty. Not enough manpower to keep anyone on him for longer."

"So, we have nothing," Tucci said. "We certainly can't chase around every one of Krups's company cars."

"No. But a GPS. We could chase a GPS." Elijah

stopped fast and grabbed his partner hard around the upper arm.

"Who out here has a GPS?"

"Abby does. Abby has a cell phone. Maybe, just maybe, she has it with her." *Oh, Lord, please let Abby have that phone with her.*

"Hey. It's worth a try. I'll get a locator on it right now." Tucci turned back to the police car. "You go ahead and talk to the kids."

The young couple sat on the ground in a patch of clover near the stable. Geoffrey stood as Elijah approached. "Are you here to find Daniel?"

Elijah nodded. "Did he say anything to either of you about leaving this afternoon? You have any idea where he might be?"

"I have no idea where he is," Kasey said as she stood from the ground and dusted her skirt. "But he was not happy to see Miss Brittney Baker at church today. And as soon as the service was over, he made a beeline for her and they exchanged a few words."

"Did you hear any of what they said?"

The kids shook their heads.

"Okay. Thanks. If you think of anything else—" Elijah started to turn away.

"Sir, I don't know if this is helpful or not. And I only just thought of it because we are at Stottlemeyers' today, but..." Geoffrey hesitated.

"What's that?"

"Well, Jessica and Daniel, they had a special place," the teen explained.

"A special place?" Elijah repeated his words just as they stirred a flowing of memories of his own special place.

"*Jah,* it was near here. In the woods somewhere, I believe."

Elijah was filled with hope again. "Yes, I know exactly the spot."

"Is it here?" Hannah walked into the shack and confronted the two arguing teens. Abigail followed in after her.

Daniel stopped feeling around the boards on the floor and looked up. Hannah still could not see his eyes below the brim of his black hat. "Mrs. Nolt, Miss Miller. You shouldn't be here. I was just telling Miss Baker that she, too, should leave. It's not safe here."

"Brittney, you should be resting," Abigail said. "I don't know how you had the strength to walk all this way."

"I knew when I saw Daniel at church that he was scared. When I saw him running into the woods, I had to come. This is all my fault. I have to fix it."

Abigail put her arm around the girl. "Here, come and sit. Rest because you will have to walk back in a bit."

"You should walk back now," Daniel said. "It's not safe here."

"Not safe?" Hannah repeated, looking around at the old wood. "Daniel, why do you think Jessica hid the journal here?"

"Well, she told me that the hiding place had something to do with you. She told Brittney the hiding place had something to do with me. I know she wouldn't lie to either of us, so I think both are true."

"This hunting cabin would make sense, then, if she brought you here." Hannah smiled.

"*Jah,* everyone was thinking this journal was at Nolt Cottage or in the stable," Daniel explained, "but this morning when we were sitting at Stottlemeyers', I thought of this place. Jessica showed it to me years ago. She said it was your special play place when she was a child. That you brought her here, Mrs. Nolt. And she brought me here, too, so…"

"Then where is it?" Brittney asked. "Daniel's right. We all need to get out of here. Krups has people watching all of you. It won't be long before they are here."

"Did you look behind that loose brick in the old fireplace?" Hannah said.

Daniel paused for a moment, then rushed over to the fireplace. He ran his hands over the rows of brick.

"Lower." Hannah also made her way to the old chimney. "Here."

She pulled away a dark brown brick. "It's this one."

Daniel reached his hand into the dark space. "There's something here." He pulled out a small quilted bag like the ones that she and Jessica used to make to sell in the local tourist shops. He opened the bag and inside was a tiny electronic device that looked like a big cell phone or a small tablet.

"That's it," Brittney said. "That's it. Recorded on it are security codes to half the buildings and accounts that belong to Krups and others."

"So much trouble just for this little piece of nothing I can hold in my hand. I would like to take a hammer to it so that it cannot hurt anyone else." Hannah took the piece from Daniel and lifted the electronic tablet. She truly wanted to smash it to pieces for all the pain it had caused her. "How does it work?"

"My stepdad said that it has a USB port and will hook up to any computer," Brittney said. "If you know the password, you can read anything on it. But only he knows the password."

"That's right, little lady," a deep voice sounded from the front of the cabin. "That's why we'll go spring your dad right after we get what we need from here. Take her to the car. And bring me the journal. Now."

Hannah, Abigail and Daniel huddled together against the fireplace. At the door was a short, gray-headed man dressed in a fine suit. He held a gun and directed two other muscular and mean-looking men with him, who also had guns.

"You can't, Krups. I won't go back to him," Brittney said. "Isn't that right, Abigail? Your brother said he wouldn't let that happen, right?"

"Get her out of here," Krups yelled. "Tie the others up."

One large man with dark, oily skin grabbed Brittney without care and slung her over his shoulder. Hannah and Abigail both cringed thinking of her bruises and how tender she must still be.

The third man was bald, angry and as strong a man as Hannah had ever seen. He snatched the journal from Hannah's hands and tossed it to Mr. Krups. He pulled a rope and knife from his pocket.

"Stand over there." He pointed them away from the fireplace.

"You look strong," he said to her. "Here. Tie up the others. Ankles and wrists."

He handed her the rope. She reached for the knife as well.

"Nice try." He laughed. "I'll cut the rope when you're ready. Thanks."

Hannah trembled as she worked the ropes around Daniel's ankles and wrists.

"Be brave," she whispered to them in their Pennsylvania Dutch. "The Lord is with us."

Tears were in the boy's eyes as she tied his ankles. "I'm sorry," he repeated. "I'm so sorry."

"Quit your yacking in German." The man waved his gun. "This is America. Speak English."

He came close, checked to see the ropes were tight, then cut the ends. "Now her."

Hannah moved around to Abigail.

Abigail stared hard at her. Her face like a stone. "Hold it," she whispered in their own tongue. "When he checks the ropes."

Hold what? Hannah's trembling fingers fumbled and she dropped the ropes to the floor.

"Hurry up." The man gave her a scolding look. "Haven't you finished tying her yet?"

Hannah picked up the rope and started to wrap it around Abigail's wrists.

"I don't know why you're going to all this trouble. It will take us thirty minutes to get back to the farm. You'll have plenty of time to get away," Hannah said.

"You're not going back to the farm, darling," he said. "You're going to have a little campfire."

Krups stomped back into the cabin. "You're taking too long."

In the one second they looked away, Abigail slipped something into Hannah's hands.

Her cell phone. Abigail had her cell phone and didn't want that brute of a man to find it.

"Leave it on," she whispered.

Hannah froze, the ropes and cell phone in her small hands. Already she could smell the cabin beginning to burn.

"Come on," Krups said again. "Just shoot them and let them burn. We got to get out of here."

Was it possible that the old hunting cabin was still there and that was where they had all gone? Elijah ran from talking to the teens toward the car to get his partner.

Tucci was already waving him to the space behind the barn.

"GPS?" he asked.

"Yep," Tucci said. "Your sister's cell phone says she's two miles into these woods. I've got a headset and device on me. Leslie back in I.T. is going to guide us through to the location."

"May not be necessary." Elijah started to run. Tucci followed. "There's a cabin back here. I thought it had been torn down long ago. But according to those kids, it's still here and Daniel and Jessica used to frequent it."

Elijah and Tucci sprinted through the woods, half going on his memory of the cabin's location, half listening to Tucci's tech speaking to him from the city.

It was difficult terrain as the path had grown over. There were many briars. And the space was thick with trees.

"Leslie says we're close," Tucci said. They slowed as they were both breathing heavily from the exertion.

"Do you smell what I smell?" he asked.

Tucci nodded. "Smoke!"

Elijah and Tucci both pulled their weapons and proceeded toward the burning cabin, which they could just now see through the thick foliage.

"They're there." Elijah made a halt motion with his hand. "There's only one door. I see one man at the car. Let's go in at the same time from opposite sides."

"Roger." Tucci took off to the right. Elijah continued to the left side of the cabin.

On the count of thirty, they both rushed the front of the cabin. Tucci aimed at the car. Elijah at the door of the cabin.

"Company!" The driver, a large dark-skinned man, got out from inside the car and aimed at Elijah. Elijah dodged the bullet while Tucci took the guy out from the back. A scream sounded from inside the car. *Brittney*.

Another man appeared at the door to the cabin. Elijah hoped there weren't many more of them. The man from the cabin ran forward to the driver of the car, who had just been shot. As he looked down, Tucci stepped out of the woods and put his gun to his head.

"Drop the weapon." Tucci slapped a pair of cuffs on the guy and pushed him to the ground.

Elijah peered into the car. Brittney was tied up in the backseat.

"Stay down," he said. "Where are the others?"

"Inside. Krups is in there."

"Any others?"

"Just those two," she said.

Tucci cuffed the man to the steering wheel, and then the two of them flanked the cabin.

On three, Elijah mouthed to his partner.

As they rushed in, Elijah prayed that Hannah and his sister were alive and well.

TWENTY

"Don't take another step." Krups held Hannah at arm's length with his fingers around her throat and a gun at her back. Less than a foot in front of her were large flames licking away at the rotted cabin.

Abigail and Daniel sat on the floor tied to each other. It was a stalemate situation. If he made a move, Hannah would get hurt or killed. Krups, on the other hand, was too arrogant to realize that he couldn't win.

"Give it up, Krups," Elijah said. "We've already got Jackson. He's going to testify against you."

"Not if he's dead, he won't."

"He's in protective custody," Tucci said. "Your claws only go so deep. You can't get to him anymore."

"We'll see about that." Angry, he pushed Hannah closer to the flames.

"No." Elijah froze, his stomach knotted with fear.

Hannah whimpered as he stretched her out over the fire.

"Back up or I'll drop her," Krups warned.

Elijah backed up. Krups relaxed his grip around Hannah's throat.

"Come on, Krups," Tucci said. "Let me get these people out of here. There's no need to harm them."

Krups seemed to consider his words. "Yes, you take those two out. Leave me with her."

Leave Hannah with him? No way.

Tucci moved quickly to release Abigail and Daniel and get them out of the smoky cabin.

"I told you to leave," Krups said, cocking his gun at Hannah's back.

"I can't leave without her." Elijah took a step closer.

"Stop. St-stop right there." Krups shook his gun. "It doesn't matter. I've got all the codes. I can change anything. Break into any system. You can't stop me. And you'll not be able to trace me, either."

"You can't get out, Krups," Elijah said, inching just a bit closer to them. "You're never going to get to use the codes."

"I will. They're mine. I've got the journal right here." Krups trembled, sweat pouring from his face. As Jackson had said, he'd gone mad.

"Let her go," Elijah said.

Krups was shaking his head; his eyes looked wild. He moved Hannah away from the flames and now had her directly between himself and Elijah.

"That's right," Elijah coaxed him. "Pass her over to me."

Elijah saw Tucci in his peripheral. His partner signaled him to go ahead with the exchange. Tucci would come up from behind and disarm him.

Finally this would all be over.

Elijah inched just a bit closer and reached out for Hannah. Krups released her and she hurried toward Elijah.

As planned, Tucci ran at Krups from behind. But Krups had anticipated him. The crazy man turned and aimed at Tucci.

As Hannah ran into his left arm, Elijah lifted his right hand and fired just a moment before Krups. Krups fell to the floor. It was all over.

Hannah was still shaking when the fire truck and emergency unit arrived. Behind them was another string of cars. Out of the first one, Thomas came running. McClendon was with him and also another man Hannah did not know.

Thomas hugged her tight. "I have prayed to God every minute that you would be safe and that

He would spare you. I'm so sorry that I have not told you the whole truth."

Hannah lifted an eyebrow. "The truth? What can you mean?"

Thomas released her and waved Elijah and the strange man over. He took Elijah's hand and patted his shoulder in a manly fashion; tears had filled his eyes. "Elijah Miller, this is Governor Derry. Mr. Derry, Detective Miller and my sister-in-law, Hannah Nolt."

Elijah shook hands with the governor. "You did this, Thomas? You arranged with the governor for me to be here?"

Thomas gave him a quick nod. "I did. And I had to keep it from *Ordnung*. I had to make it sound as if you had to be here."

The governor pumped Elijah's hand, then kissed Hannah's. "Mr. Miller, you and your partner have stopped what was about to be the biggest breach of security in American history. I cannot thank you enough. I'll be in touch with you both very soon."

With that, Derry returned to his large blue car and left. Chief McClendon and his men worked the scene, taping the area, taking pictures, removing the two bodies. Brittney was taken to the hospital. It was enough activity to make Hannah's already-spinning head explode. She turned to Thomas and

Elijah. "You two seem to be okay with all of this, but would one of you please explain?"

Thomas hugged her again. "Jessica asked to borrow my cell phone the day before she died. She was nervous. Not like herself. When I saw her body the next day, I knew that she had gotten mixed up in something bad. I knew we needed help. Governor Derry had said to let him know if I ever needed a favor and so I told him about Jessica and the phone call. And that our people would not allow an investigation. But I thought of Elijah and I knew that if anyone could get in here and ask questions and protect us, it would be him. I asked Mr. Derry if he could somehow get you here."

"You could have called me yourself, Thomas," Elijah said.

"I see that now," Thomas said. "But I was worried at first about your response, and about what the elders might say."

"Why didn't you tell me about the phone call?" Hannah asked.

"It was untraceable. And you were feeling bad enough about things."

"But why not tell Elijah? Why act like you didn't want him here?"

"I did want him here. But I didn't want him courting and confusing you and leaving again." Thomas shrugged. "And as I said, I did not want any trouble with the elders. I did not think they would look upon my calling the governor too kindly. And McClendon said the phone call wouldn't help you out."

"It wouldn't have," Elijah said. "Real photos and the clothing—"

Hannah reached up and touched both their shoulders. "It's over. Let us not second-guess ourselves."

"You are right, sister," Thomas hugged her once more. Then the police working the scene asked him to step back.

Hannah could hardly remember the rest of what happened. The fire was put out. Another ambulance took Tucci to the hospital. The bullet Krups had fired in his direction had grazed his leg. Thomas and Abigail had left to speak to the People. They would meet and pray and part of her longed to be among them. It was late when Elijah drove her back to Nolt Cottage.

She sat in his car not wanting to get out and say goodbye. Elijah would not be back and they both knew it. They would both go back to their own worlds now. Now that the terror was over.

"How long will your partner be out?" she asked him.

"Not long," he said. "The bullet didn't hit anything important."

There was silence between them and she sensed

his inner struggle over having taken a life. "It's not for me to judge, Elijah. But if you ask me, I think you did the right thing. The man you killed would have shot again, then turned and shot the both of us. David killed Goliath with a stone, did he not? It is not our way to choose violence but today it was forced on us. You stood your ground. That is also Amish thinking."

Elijah's lips turned up slightly at the corners. "I appreciate your words more than you know."

"What will happen to Brittney?" she asked, looking away, afraid that if she saw his tender blue eyes, she would not be able to finish, not be able to say goodbye.

"She's with Child Services," Elijah said. "In any case, she turns eighteen in a few weeks. I think Abigail offered for her to come and stay with her. What she really wants is to find her mother that Jackson beat and ran off. We have some people with the FBI working on that for her. And the codes are safely back at Dutch Confidential."

"Thank you, Elijah," she said. "Thank you for coming. For helping me find out about Jessica. It was so good to see you and see what you do. After having a gun at my back, I understand your desire to protect others. I understand why you were driven to leave Willow Trace and become a detective."

He looked deep into her eyes and took her hand. "That wasn't the only reason I left."

So, now he finally opens up about the past? Now that he was leaving. Hannah sighed hard. "I would not have been happy outside of the faith. You know that."

"I would have stayed for you."

She glanced away but left her hand in his, enjoying the warmth of his touch. "But I couldn't give you what you wanted, Elijah. I chose Peter because that was the only way we could both be happy and have what we wanted."

"I wanted you, Hannah," he said. "I still do, God help me. But you have Thomas. He's a good man. You will be loved and happy here. You did the right thing. I am not Plain. Especially after today. I showed that to everyone." He started to open the door and get out of the car.

"You mean because of using your weapon against Krups?"

He nodded. "Yes, I didn't make good on my promise to my *Dat,* that I wouldn't use my gun."

"But didn't you also promise to serve and protect?"

"I did. But *Dat* will never understand that. In any case, Hannah, I couldn't stand to be here and see you wed to yet another man. I won't be back again." He got out of the car. She could tell he was choked with emotion as he walked around to open her door. "Come on. I'll walk you in and say goodbye to Thomas."

"I won't be marrying Thomas." She took his hand as she stepped out of his fancy car. "We don't love each other that way. He's my brother. Nothing more."

"You say that now, Hannah. But..."

"It's true. I talked to your sister about it. Ask her."

He shook his head. "It won't matter. I can't come back. My actions today only sealed that fate. I don't belong here. You know it."

"I don't know it, Elijah. I think that was true of you when you were younger. You wanted to go out and help the world, but now I think you want something else."

"Hannah, you're only making this harder. I know you've wanted to talk about the past and about us. But can't you see? There is no us."

"Then, at least, let me finish telling you what happened back then." His harsh words brought tears to her eyes. But she was determined to tell him the whole truth.

"I cannot have children, Elijah. When I was eighteen, I had a tumor. It was removed and with it went all my possibilities to be a mother. Peter happened on my mother and me as we were leaving the hospital. He saw me in the wheelchair and of course he came and asked. So I told him

I could never have children. He could see that I was devastated. That's when he asked me to marry him. So that I could be a mother. So, yes, I chose Peter because I chose Jessica. I chose him because he could make me a mother. I chose him because I could not make you a father."

Elijah stepped back around the car door. She couldn't read his expression. Shock, pity, anger, sadness. Whatever was there, he kept it all hidden behind his steely blue eyes.

Then he looked away and she saw the pain on his face—the one thing she had never wanted to give him.

"You chose well, Hannah," he whispered, close to her ear. "Peter and Jessica were blessed to have you in their lives." He leaned over and kissed the top of her head. "You chose well, Hannah Nolt."

He walked her to the front door, gave her hand a squeeze and then turned. "Take care of yourself."

She watched him from the front porch as he drove away and out of her life again.

TWENTY-ONE

Two months later

Elijah filed away the last of the Mason-Hendricks case paperwork and shut down his computer. He wanted a drink of water, but instead of walking to the cooler he stayed at his desk running his finger around and around the rim of a coffee cup in a continuous circular motion. His thoughts fixed on things far, far away from the Philadelphia Police Internal Affairs Department.

A hand waved in front of his face, breaking his trance. It was Tucci standing before him, hands on hips with that I-know-what-you're-thinking-about-again look on his face.

"Sorry," Elijah said, sitting up tall, trying to feign interest in whatever it was his partner had come to tell him. "Did you say something?"

"Would it matter?" Tucci lifted an eyebrow.

"Yes, Mitchie. It matters. I don't know why I can't focus these days," he said.

"Really? You don't know?" There was an edge of playful sarcasm in his words. "Let me help you. Her name starts and ends with the same letter."

"Yeah, well…Hannah and I have said goodbye for the last time. She's happy the way things are. And I'm happy here. This is where I belong."

"Yeah, you're Mr. Sunshine these days." Tucci pulled up a chair and sat in front of his friend. "Why don't you just go back and talk to her? See how she feels about you? Wouldn't that be better than sitting around here wondering all the time?"

"Come on. I explained it to you before. There's no place for Hannah and me. She belongs there and I—well, I don't know where I belong but it's not in Willow Trace. Anyway, my father doesn't want me back. He made that very clear."

"So, I guess you don't want to talk to him, then?"

"My father? Like he wants to talk to me. Ha, ha. Right."

"Well, he's here. And he's not asking to see anyone else."

"*Dat* is here? In the Philadelphia Police Department?" Elijah stood and looked toward the reception. Just beyond the door he could see him, his father, pacing back and forth.

Tucci stood and motioned toward the door.

Preacher Miller stepped through dressed in his Sunday best, black trousers, white shirt, black hat, suspenders. He made his way toward the center of the room where Elijah stood, mouth half-opened in disbelief.

"Father. I—I—"

"No, son, it is I who have come to do the talking today." His father spread his feet, leaned back on his heels and placed a hand firmly on Elijah's shoulder. "Let me speak."

Elijah nodded, his eyes fixed toward the floor. Even though he was not sure he could bear to hear any more harsh words, especially in front of his colleagues. Most likely, his father had come to deliver a formal statement, something kin to a shunning. He'd been waiting for it. Possibly that was why he hadn't gone back to face Hannah and his inescapable feelings for her. Now he was glad he had stayed away from Willow Trace.

"What I have to say is simple," he continued. "The elders have decided that it is unfair to punish you for using your weapon when you, in fact, have never taken your vows to the church. You are in no way required to follow our beliefs. I was wrong to speak so harshly to you. You are welcome to come home anytime. To visit. Or to stay, should you find yourself called to join the church. That would be a most pleasing event to your mother and me. In either case, Elijah, I am proud of you. You chose a different path than I wanted for you, but on it you have made a good life and you have become a good man. I am as proud as any father could be."

"Is this true, Father? I am welcome to join the church?"

"If you feel this is where the Lord has called you, yes."

"It is." Elijah nodded. "I want to come home."

Hannah wiped down the exam table and instruments in Abigail's clinic with a mixture of alcohol and water. It was five o'clock and Abigail had no more midwife appointments for the day. In fact, Abigail and Brittney had taken the horse and buggy to the butcher's to fetch some lamb for a stew, and Hannah, instead of joining them, was able to enjoy a delectable moment of solitude. Life with Abigail Miller didn't allow for many of them. There were always so many people coming and going. And much more conversation than Hannah had ever been a part of at the Nolts'.

Which was why she did not jump when a knock sounded at the door after hours, a "walk-in" patient, Abigail called those without an appointment.

"Coming." Hannah put away the cleaning rag and checked to see that her hair was still tightly tucked away in her *Kapp*. She pressed the white apron with her hands and opened the front door. "Miss Miller is not in at the moment. You are welcome to…"

She stopped, seeing as the man at the door was most likely not a patient. In fact, it was Elijah and he was dressed in Plain clothes and was clean-shaven. He looked so different that it had taken Hannah all of that time to realize who he was.

"I take it from the expression on your face that Abby didn't tell you I was coming to call on you," he said in a sort of apologetic tone.

"I—I um, no. She did not." *To call on me?* Hannah was sure she had misunderstood. After all, her heart was beating so loudly she could barely manage to speak over the pounding. She must gain control of herself before she embarrassed herself yet again with him. "Abigail went to Mr. Hochenlooper's. She's not been gone long. I'm sure if you hurry you can catch her."

Elijah removed his black hat and twirled it in his fingers. "Well, this is a lousy beginning if I have to explain more than once that I've come to call on *you,* Hannah Nolt. I have not come for a visit with my sister. I've come to see you and ask if you will take a ride with me on this fine night. I'll have you home early. I already promised my sister I would. Not a minute past ten."

Hannah frowned. Was he kidding? She had

heard that he had come to stay with his father a few weeks ago. But for how long? Did he think he could simply change his clothes and shave and that would put them in the same world? "No, Elijah. I cannot. My place is here with the People."

"And so is mine." Elijah stepped forward and took her hand. "I've come home. I have my father's blessing. I've been working in his mill. I bought the old abandoned Manders' place and I'm fixing it up. It will take a while, but I've got time. I'm not to join the church until the spring. Until then, I can call on you and once I've taken my vows, well…if you'll have me, Hannah Kurtz Nolt, I'd like to be your husband soon after."

"But will you be happy giving up your police work? Will you be satisfied knowing you can never have children?"

"Once I saw you again, I knew there was only one place I could ever be happy," he said, pulling her hand to his lips. "Beside you."

Hannah smiled, every happy emotion swirling inside her so much so that she felt she might burst from it. "In that case, I'll just fetch my wrap and leave your sister a note."

Elijah smiled wide at her consent and grabbed her round the waist, lifting her and spinning her in a circle. "And might I start our outing with a sweet kiss?"

Hannah laughed with joy and threw her arms

around his strong neck. He stopped spinning her and pulled her in to his lips for what she hoped to be the first of many, many kisses.

* * * * *

Dear Reader,

The Amish people and their culture have long fascinated me. It started because I have relatives who live in Lancaster County. When I was a child, we visited the area every summer, staying with my aunt, while my uncle traveled as visiting professor in various German universities. Interestingly, it was also there my love and addiction to books germinated, for my uncle has a collection in his home that would rival any public library. I loved roaming through his stacks and wondering how a person could fit all those stories and facts into his brain. In fact, I often wondered how the floor of his study didn't give way with the weight of all those books and go crashing into the living room below.

In any case, it was also during these visits that I had my first encounters with the Amish. I remember even then—at the ripe age of seven or eight—questioning the paradox of their self-sufficient communities surrounded by and yet cut off from the modern world around them. We could see them, talk to them, walk on their farms and buy their homemade products, but we couldn't feel who they were. They belonged to another place all their own and even though we stood side by side, I had no connection and no understanding of them.

As I began to create this story, I had high hopes of uncovering their mysticism through my "adult" wisdom and being able to walk away from the experience of writing this novel with a complete and thorough knowledge of the Amish. But that did not happen. The more I peered into the Amish world, the more I realized its infinite complexities. Their lifestyles are called Plain and Simple, but as individuals, I believe, they are as unique and intricate as snowflakes.

To that end, I hope you enjoyed this visit to Willow Trace and the story of Hannah and Elijah, where big-city danger threatens the safe haven of this isolated (and fictitious) Amish community.

In Christ's Love,
Kit

Questions for Discussion

1. When she was eighteen, do you think Hannah was right in choosing Peter and Jessica even when she still had strong romantic feelings for Elijah?

2. Elijah is a bit like the Prodigal Son in this story. Discuss the estranged relationship between Eli and his father. Why is it so hard for either of them to face each other? And to forgive each other?

3. Who is your favorite character in the story? Why?

4. What do you think will happen to Brittney once her stepfather is convicted? Do you think she truly wanted to become a part of the Amish community? Or do you think she will search for her mother? Maybe even return to the wrong side of the tracks? How would you end her story?

5. Do you think Elijah would have returned to Willow Trace eventually even if Hannah had not needed him? Why or why not?

6. Hannah is conflicted and afraid to discover

the truth of what happened to Jessica. Which of her emotions do you feel would be the strongest—her guilt at feeling that she didn't accept God's will, her fear of learning that her stepdaughter had done something bad, her desire to know the truth or her grief?

7. Amish teens are often portrayed on TV and in literature as truly exploiting their freedoms in the time of *Rumspringa*. Discuss how accurate you believe this "Hollywood" image to be. Do you think in this story that Hannah should have been stricter with Jessica or that she did the right thing by trusting her stepdaughter to make wise choices? For any parent, where and when do we allow our kids to make their own mistakes?

8. What is your favorite scene in the book and why?

9. Amish strive to be separate from the world in a very physical sense by not having power lines or telephone lines connected to their homes. They do, however, in a few communities (not all) allow the use of cell phones and oil-powered electricity for certain, specific tasks. Discuss how technology has changed everyone's lifestyles over the past twenty, ten

and five years. Do you feel that technology makes your life simpler or more complicated?

10. How do you see Hannah and Elijah ten years into the future? How does Eli adapt to coming home? How does Hannah deal with his outside experiences?

11. Which aspects of Amish life do you find appealing? Which are not so appealing?

12. Hannah let go of Elijah when she was young, partly because she couldn't part with Jessica, whom she'd raised as her own since birth, but also because she believed Elijah wanted a family that she couldn't give him. Have you ever cared for a person whom you've had to let go? What were the circumstances? Did the relationship end on good terms? Why or why not?

13. If Hannah had told Elijah the truth about her infertility as a teen, do you think she and Elijah would have stayed together? If so, where would they have lived? Inside or outside the Amish community? Why?

14. Brittney thinks she wants to live in the Amish community. Elijah left the Amish community and then returned. Have you ever

lived in a different culture? For how long?
How did it feel? Was it harder to leave or to
return home?

LARGER-PRINT BOOKS!

**GET 2 FREE
LARGER-PRINT NOVELS
PLUS 2 FREE
MYSTERY GIFTS**

Love Inspired
SUSPENSE
RIVETING INSPIRATIONAL ROMANCE

Larger-print novels are now available...

LARGER-PRINT BOOKS!

GET 2 FREE LARGER-PRINT NOVELS PLUS 2 FREE MYSTERY GIFTS

Larger-print novels are now available...